ACCEPTING FATE

Changing Roles Series, Book 6

JET MASTERS

ELLIE MASTERS

JEM Publishing

Copyright © 2019 Ellie Masters
EMBRACING FATE
All rights reserved.

This copy is intended for the original purchaser of this print book ONLY. No part of this print book may be reproduced, scanned, transmitted, or distributed in any printed, mechanical, or electronic form without prior written permission from Jet & Ellie Masters or JEM Publishing except in the case of brief quotations embodied in critical articles or reviews. This book is licensed for your personal enjoyment only. Please do not participate in or encourage piracy of copyrighted materials in violation of the author's rights. This book may not be re-sold or given away to other people. If you would like to share this book with another person, please purchase an additional copy for each person you share it with. If you are reading this book and did not purchase it, or it was not purchased for your use only, then you should return it to the seller and purchase your own copy. Thank you for respecting the author's work.

Image/art disclaimer: Licensed material is being used for illustrative purposes only. Any person depicted in the licensed material is a model.

Editor: Erin Toland

Proofreader: Rox Leblanc

Published in the United States of America by

JEM Publishing

This is a work of fiction. While reference might be made to actual historical events or existing locations, the names, characters, businesses, places, and incidents are either the product of the author's imagination or are used fictitiously, and any resemblance to actual persons, living or dead, business establishments, events, or locales is entirely coincidental.

ISBN: 978-1-952625-78-7

Warning

This story contains adult material and might be considered offensive to some readers.

This book is for sale to adults ONLY, as defined by the laws of the country where you made your purchase. Please store your files wisely and where they cannot be accessed by underage readers.

To My Readers

This book is a work of fiction. It does not exist in the real world and should not be construed as reality. As in most romantic fiction, I've taken liberties. Take more time in your romance and learn who you're giving a piece of your heart to. Move with caution and always protect yourself.

Be honest about your needs, your expectations, and your limits, especially if you have any triggers. Never allow your partner to violate the trust you put into their hands. Always remember, it's your responsibility to talk to them, no matter how frightening that might be.

In return, you must listen to what your partner has to say and understand their limits, as you do your own. Share your hopes, desires, and deepest, darkest secrets. Most of all, don't be afraid to seek out who you are, become what you want, and share your journey with your partner.

Jet

Books by Jet Masters

The DARKER SIDE[1]
Jet Masters is the darker side of the Jet & Ellie writing duo!

Romantic Suspense
Changing Roles Series:
THIS SERIES MUST BE READ IN ORDER.
Book 1: Command Me
Book 2: Control Me
Book 3: Collar Me
Book 4: Embracing FATE
Book 5: Seizing FATE
Book 6: Accepting FATE

HOT READS
A STANDALONE NOVEL.
Down the Rabbit Hole

Light BDSM Romance
The Ties that Bind

EACH BOOK IN THIS SERIES CAN BE READ AS A STANDALONE AND IS ABOUT A DIFFERENT COUPLE WITH AN HEA.

Alexa
Penny
Michelle
Ivy

HOT READS
Becoming His Series
THIS SERIES MUST BE READ IN ORDER.
Book 1: The Ballet
Book 2: Learning to Breathe
Book 3: Becoming His

Dark Captive Romance
A STANDALONE NOVEL.
She's MINE

---

1. Disclaimer: Books previously published under Ellie Masters

Chapter 1

Josh

I WAS GOING TO KILL HIM FOR BARGING IN ON US.

That's all I could think of while I smiled and shook Carson's hand. He intruded on something precious. Something which never should have been shared with anyone. Clara deserved better than that.

It was my fault. I fucked up, unable to keep my dick in my pants until I could fuck the love of my life someplace private. It had been a risk, but I thought we had time before our visitors arrived.

Now I paid for my impulsiveness and Clara suffered for it. She did not deserve to be put on display. Not like that.

If Carson didn't stop leering at her, it was going to cost the fucker.

First things first, we had a show to put on. A monster to entertain and innocents to save.

I hated this fucking job.

We shook and measured each other's worth in the strength of our grip.

In that exchange, I came out on top, but I did so with a healthy respect for Carson. More than two decades my senior, the man was fit and strong. I stepped between him, blocking Clara as best I could, while she took her place on the floor.

There would be no way to shield her from his depraved gaze. My attempt was laughable because she would be the centerpiece of our evening's events. At least until Kate was brought out.

"I'm looking forward to your demonstration tonight." Carson craned his neck, looking around me as Clara knelt on the floor.

"Of course, make yourself comfortable. Xavier has arranged entertainment, and I have a slave to tie up."

"More?" Carson rubbed his hands together. "You're an animal."

If he only knew. The beast within me prowled with frustration, but now wasn't the time to let it loose.

"I practice the art form of Shibari. Are you familiar with it?"

"Oh…" His disappointment twisted my guts.

Did he think I would take Clara in front of him? One look into his depraved face and my question was answered.

"It seems a lot of effort, to be honest, when you can just chain them down."

"You're obviously not a connoisseur."

We were measuring each other out, trading veiled insults; polite conversation which was anything but.

"Anyone can fuck an unwilling slave," I said. "True control is taking one who's unwilling and bending them to your will." I gestured to the couches. "Here, take a seat and see what I mean."

"You mentioned entertainment." He coughed into his fist. "Is that the extent of the evening's entertainment? Watching you tie granny knots?"

Bastard.

I smiled. "Shibari requires intense focus. Not everyone is able to appreciate the artistry behind it. This is something I enjoy. While we wait for the others, and for our main event to begin, Xavier will have other entertainment brought in. You can enjoy that while I tie my granny knots, but I think it's a useful demonstration for what a true Master can achieve. Brute force has its place, but true mastery requires finesse. Go ahead and have a seat. Xavier's slaves will be here shortly."

Carson's face twisted in a grimace, but he didn't volley back with a reply to my bald-faced insult. He smoothed his features and glanced at the couches.

"Xavier always has the best slaves, a bit rough and untrained, but that's what makes it fun."

"An untrained slave is wasted potential."

"Perhaps. Your slave is impressive." He spoke as if he were judging a show horse. "No hesitation. Quite willing. I'd even say eager? And no restraints." His admiration seemed honest, despite the veiled sneer in his tone. "I'd say she had no idea about your proclivities but then I recognize her from before. She's either a horny cunt or doing her best to make sure she's not next."

"There is something tantalizing about forcing a woman against her will, but my tastes have matured over the years. It's easy to force a slave, but far from challenging. Much more satisfying when they come to you willingly."

"And how do you do that? Use fear as a weapon? Tell her she's next on the chopping block if not perfectly well-behaved?"

"Fear is a powerful motivator, but not sufficient to instill loyalty. Not to mention it's a blunt instrument."

"Then how do you do it?"

"I make them fall in love with me."

"You're fucking kidding me." His eyes about bugged out of his head. "I expected some kind of exaggeration, but not that."

"It's no lie." I snapped my fingers. "Slave, do you love me?"

Clara's head snapped up. Her eyes rounded with fear, but her voice rang steady, true, and without hesitation.

"Yes, Sir."

It almost sounded real. God, I loved everything about Clara; her strength being but one of many things.

I made an exaggerated gesture, waving in her general direction. It was both dismissive and encompassing, as if I really did own her every thought and undying loyalty.

"Perfect obedience and absolute devotion. That is what I prefer. What about you? Have you ever had a slave who loved you?"

I knew the answer to that by the scowl on his face.

"We're not here to discuss my history with slaves. I use them and discard them when they no longer amuse me. That's all the cunts are worth."

"You're correct. We're not here to discuss how we keep our slaves. Our business is of a more…disposable nature."

"Exactly, and I have to say I'm not convinced you have something worth selling."

"Have a seat. I'm not ready to discuss business. Sit back, relax, and enjoy the show." I turned back to Clara. "I have a slave to tie up."

"Shibari," he said with a sneer. "I don't get the fascination."

"Perhaps you've never seen it performed by a Master."

"And you are?"

"I've studied it for years."

"And where did you do that? In prison?"

"As a matter of fact…" I wasn't going to share the details of my life with this waste of a human, but he needed to understand the kind of man I was. "I learned from a Thai Master. It was the only thing which kept me sane."

"Ah, your incarceration overseas."

"Yes, that was the first time I killed for pleasure." *Let that juicy morsel sink in, you bastard.* The comment held more truth than I would like.

"Ah, now that's interesting, I'd love to hear more."

"There's not much more to tell. I was young and careless. I've learned a thing or two since then; things which create opportunities we can both benefit from."

Carson took a seat in one of the plush couches. "Color me intrigued. I'd love to hear more."

The heavy wooden doors swung open. Xavier entered with Chambers, Abrams, and two men I didn't know.

"Good evening gentlemen, apologies for keeping you waiting." Xavier gave a half bow as he swept into the room. "Josh, you know Ben Chambers, but let me introduce you to his business partner, Mel Abrams. They run their resort together. Mel is in charge of security and tech."

I reached out to shake with Abrams. Our little show had officially begun.

"Nice to meet you. I hope you enjoy this evening's presentation."

Abrams shared a look with Chambers. "I am told it's unique."

"Definitely unique." I turned to the other two men who had to be Carson's associates.

Xavier introduced them. "This is Peter Stolm and Chris Standis. Good evening, Zane, nice to see you again."

The tightening of Carson's jaw didn't escape me with Xavier's use of his first name. Tension swirled between these men, not that it came as a surprise. Xavier owned Carson's only daughter.

I didn't fully understand everything behind that exchange, but something told me Raven's mother had likely been one of the slaves Carson had discarded once she served her purpose.

Xavier took over as host, relieving me from that burden. This freed me to turn my attention to Clara who had been ignored during the entire meet and greet.

I stepped to her as one of the small side doors opened behind me. A bevy of slaves, dressed in harem outfits, entered and approached the men. Sultry music began to play. Two of the women began gyrating in front of the men, while the others approached them.

Carson took no time in unbuckling his pants and unzipping his fly. He had his flaccid cock in his hand before the woman playing the part of slave knelt before him. Peter Stolm and Chris Standis followed Carson's lead, while Chambers and Abrams waved off the two women sent to them.

Xavier took a seat in one of the chairs.

"Where's your slave?" Carson guided the slave onto his cock then sat back with an exaggerated sigh.

"Your daughter is sick. Puking her guts out. I'm afraid she won't be joining us."

Carson gestured to one of the dancing slaves. "Good thing there's plenty to go around."

"I'm good, but thank you. I've heard about Josh's skill with the rope. I'm interested in a demonstration. It might be something fun to learn."

"I don't have the patience for shit like that," Carson said. "We should skip ahead to the main event."

"And miss the talents of this latest batch of slaves?" Xavier looked insulted. "I've been working with Chambers to train them. If they pass this test tonight, they'll be moving on."

"Moving on?" Carson arched a brow.

"To our resort." Abrams, a man of few words, answered. "Business has been better than ever imagined. With Xavier's training techniques, our customers are insanely happy. Word is getting around."

"I'm sure it has." Carson grabbed a fistful of the woman's hair and slammed her up and down his cock. Her slurping sounds filled the room and Carson continued talking as if he were in the middle of a business meeting rather than getting his dick sucked. "Xavier's techniques are impressive, although it seems he may have some competition."

"No competition." I held a length of rope in my hands, measuring out the sections I would use. "I'm not interested in training any slave but mine."

"I have a question about tonight's entertainment," Carson asked. "Does she know?"

"Kate Summers?"

"Of course." Carson was a pig. It disgusted me that he talked to me while getting his dick sucked off.

"Does she know what?"

"That you killed her office assistant?"

I gave a low laugh. "Kate watched the live video feed. She knows exactly what happened and what I have planned. I've been letting her stew, waiting for tonight. I told you I wanted her to suffer. Every day, I leave that video looping in her cell."

Carson chuckled. "Now that is sadism at its finest. I can't wait for the main event." Moving seamlessly from discussing Kate's impending death to letting his orgasm roll through him, Carson leaned his head back and came with a groan.

The pig disgusted me, and if it were up to me, he'd leave this event with a knife buried in his chest. Unfortunately, he remained useful to us for now. That meant I couldn't kill him.

Lucky bastard.

I turned my attention to Clara while the men entertained themselves with the slaves.

"What is your color, my sweet Clara?"

"Yellow."

She had two colors she could use during our scenes, green and red. Green for go. Red for problem. We learned together, testing tolerances and limits. Not once had she ever given a response other than green.

"Yellow?"

She bit her lower lip and kept her voice low so that we weren't overheard. "I'm trying not to *jump*, but I've never been this scared."

Her comment was not lost on me, nor its reference to the Island of Conclusions. I pressed our foreheads together and brushed my nose against hers.

"Trust in me. I know it's hard, but I need you to trust me."

She gave the tiniest of nods. "I will try."

"What color?" I wouldn't proceed without a green. I would never force her to do anything against her will.

Never again.

Her voice returned shaky, but true. "Green."

"Good girl." I tried to reassure her. "You can close your eyes if you need to, or I can use a hood."

She shook her head. "No hood, please."

"As you wish." I held out my hand.

She took it, and I helped her to her feet. I'd practiced this particular pose and could do the knots in my sleep.

I leaned in and brushed my lips over hers. "I will not fail you."

And so, our evening began.

Chapter 2

Josh

I began my rope work, as always, by taking in a few slow, deep breaths. This time would be different from all the others. Before now, exploration and perfection guided my hands. I had to learn Clara's body, getting to know the rhythms of how she responded to my touch. The need to achieve perfection kept me laser-focused and on task.

Exploration and perfection were not my goals now.

There was an audience and this was a performance.

While Clara and I might not be the focus of their attention with the slave girls present, we remained under a microscope, nonetheless. While Carson reinvigorated his flaccid cock, his penetrating gaze watched my every move. It was too intense. Too inquisitive. I wanted to blind the fucker for staring at my girl, but this was necessary.

He needed to see Clara's absolute devotion.

For the most part, he ignored his business associates who were getting their dicks sucked. A woman gyrated over Chambers, and Abrams had a girl beside him. He made a show of feeling her up. Xavier was the only one without a woman.

He and Carson traded hostile glares while a length of rope

passed through my hands.

"Still green?" I checked in with Clara.

With the basic harness nearly complete, I worked on the ties which bent Clara's forward knee. Once I began, she would need to balance on one leg. A difficult feat, it was made bearable with her hands resting on my shoulders. I loved that contact and her dependence on me.

"Yes, Sir." Her breathy reply indicated she had slipped into a meditative space.

The feel of her hands on me never failed to stir a reaction. My dick lengthened, tenting the fabric of my pants as I worked. This was not a pose for fucking. It was pure artistry, enforcing the submissive's complete reliance on her Master as ropes wrapped around her body and limited her movement. Nevertheless, I wanted to slip inside of her. Now that I'd had a taste of her sweet pussy, I needed more. I didn't think I'd ever have enough.

The thought of her being helpless in a room filled with depraved men did not sit well with me, but there was nothing to do about that.

Sounds of sex filled the room as the men took their pleasure. I tuned all of it out, working quickly to finish this part of the evening.

With her left leg bent and bound, I turned my attention to her arms. One would sweep out behind her while the other lifted gracefully overhead. I reinforced the main scaffolding of rope which would bear her weight, double checking all the important pressure points.

"Are you ready?" To complete my work, it was time to lift her into the air.

"Yes, Sir."

"Do you trust me?"

"I do." Deep in a trancelike state, her answers came as single words and short sentences.

"Do you forgive me?" I pressed my lips to hers, seeking the connection we shared.

Carson may have walked in on us, but I refused to let that ruin what had been the best, most intimate, sexual experience of my life.

Something had shifted within me, a reverence for what we'd shared, and intense appreciation for the trust she extended.

I deserved none of it.

"Always," she said.

It would be nice if that were true, but Clara didn't know all my secrets. I would share them with her. She deserved to know the kind of man she extended her trust toward. My fear was that she would revoke everything once she understood I was very much the monster she feared.

A killer.

A rapist.

There was no redemption for a man like me.

I pulled on the ropes attached to the ring overhead, and slowly, gracefully, Clara rose into the air. Her lower leg dangled, and her right arm rested by her side.

I went to work attaching the ropes which would connect her arm and leg, measuring out the precise lengths which would turn all this loose rope into a work of art once I tied her ankle to the support behind her.

Clara's eyes closed as I manipulated her body.

Completely helpless, and at my mercy, she surrendered to it all. When I placed the last rope and tied the last knot, I took two steps back to admire her.

A thing of beauty, she slowly twirled in the air. One leg swept out behind her, an arm trailed behind with it, while her front leg arced forward in mid-leap. Her other arm curved gracefully overhead. I had even tied in her hair, letting it sweep backward to continue the movement.

Carson came to stand beside me, and I resisted the urge to block him.

"I was wrong," he said.

"Excuse me?"

"I thought all of this was a waste of time. Is she in subspace?"

A look of contentment spread across Clara's face, smoothing out her features and highlighting her beauty.

"The entire practice is a meditative experience for both the slave and Master. I find it brings us together on a different plane."

"Sounds like metaphysical bullshit."

"I once thought the same thing. Fortunately, I'm open-minded. You should consider trying it out. If you enjoy control, there's nothing that tops this."

"I think a whip and crop do just fine."

"Again with the blunt tools."

He tensed beside me.

"Don't get me wrong."

I tried to ease some of the negative energy between us. I couldn't win this man over if we were constantly at odds.

"There's nothing more delicious than the screams of a slave beneath my whip, but that's control by force." I gestured toward Clara. "This is surrender by choice."

"Interesting."

"Once you have a taste of that, it changes everything."

"If you say so, and speaking of the other, when do we begin?"

I glanced at Xavier and waved him over. He would stand guard over Clara until Jake returned with Kate. Clara's guards, Chad and Bay, would make their entrance with Jake, dragging a struggling Kate to her *'doom.'*

For the next hour, I would watch everything unfold from a secret room and try my best to resist the urge to protect my sweet Clara.

"Is it time?" Xavier made a show of examining Clara.

"Your business associate is getting antsy," I said.

"Not antsy, but ready to move things along," Carson said.

"Well, take your seat then." I rubbed my hands on my trousers. "The bitch has been stewing long enough. I'll be right back."

Xavier gestured back to the couches. "Can I get you anything else?"

"No, I'm good."

As I retreated, I couldn't help but overhear Carson as he whined.

"It's about time we get this show on the road."

"Are you that eager?"

"Your friend is crazy if he thinks he can pull this off. I'm just here to watch. Honestly, I'm surprised you're involved at all."

"I follow the money. You have an operation which caters to a similar demographic which, I understand, brings in a healthy profit. Men like us always find those willing to pay to indulge their darker cravings."

"What's his interest in my business?"

"Not your business as much as your client list."

"That's not something I share."

"He's not looking to take it, but rather provide a service, one you will benefit from."

"Then why aren't you going into business with him?"

"Who says I'm not?"

The rest of their conversation faded as I exited the room. The heavy wooden doors shut behind me, and I picked up my pace. In less than a minute, I scanned my retina and entered Command and Control.

Kate glanced up. "That shit is a piece of work."

"You don't say." I crossed my arms. "Are you ready?"

My attention shifted to my identical twin who stood behind Kate. The makeup artists had been hard at work placing bruises on her body. Knowing my brother's tastes, some of those were probably real and had been put there by his hand.

"As much as possible." He placed a hand on Kate's shoulder.

Kate had a bruise around her eye. Cuts along her jawline and temple. Her arms and wrists were heavily bruised. I couldn't see the rest of her body.

The thin silver scar across her neck glistened in the light of the fluorescent bulbs.

Initially, the plan had been to build up that area and place a blood reservoir beneath it. Her neck was supposed to be sliced, thus enacting my revenge, but the special effects team ran into difficulties. She could be cut there, and blood would flow, but Jake would strangle her instead.

I had intended on her being nude for the whole thing, thinking it would have the greatest impact. Jake refused.

Kate would be whipped fully clothed. His uncanny precision

would strip her in front of the audience, lending realism to the entire show. Beneath her shirt, more bruises waited to be unveiled, but he would lay down actual welts before strangling her.

Kate's screams would be real, as would be her death.

Joining us in the ready room was Forest's medical team: his sister Skye, Tia Meyers, and Ryker Lyons.

It would be up to those three to bring Kate back to life.

The timing had to be perfect.

Skye handed Kate a tiny capsule.

"Keep this in your cheek, then crack it open when…" She swallowed thickly, "after Jake strangles you."

"I got it."

Jake glanced at me and the muscles of his jaw bunched. From here on out, both Kate and Clara's safety would be in his hands.

Kate spun around. "I guess it's time."

Chad and Bay, who had been standing silently along the far wall, took a step forward. Chad grasped a long pole. Bay had a set of iron cuffs.

My gut twisted as they approached Kate. She obediently turned and lifted her hands up. Chad lay the pole behind her head, along her shoulders, while Bay locked the cuffs around her wrists and secured them to the rings on the pole.

Meanwhile, I stripped.

We'd discussed how Jake and I would switch places. The easiest thing would be to wear identical clothing. No one would be the wiser, but then Jake mentioned blood splatter. There would be no way to mimic any of Kate's blood.

Jake removed his clothing and dressed as I handed him my shirt and then my pants. He said nothing the entire time. A reluctant participant, he hated every bit of this plan. That was fine by me.

I didn't care what he thought. The rift between us would likely remain for the rest of our lives, and his forgiveness wasn't something I could force. Not that it mattered. I didn't need him to forgive me.

All that remained was to make things square with Wu. Through my negligence, his daughter died. Whatever it took, I would save his twins.

Chapter 3

Clara

Rope bound me.

Suspended me.

Embraced me.

I twirled in a room designed to inflict pain, and yet I found myself wrapped in Josh's protection. He may have left temporarily, but his touch encircled me with every inch of rope wound around my body.

I was in bliss.

Master Xavier stood beside me. I sensed Josh's hand in that. He placed Xavier there to watch over me.

But where did My Monster go?

If I flexed my muscles, I could rock gently, maybe even spin a little. Normally, I did that, enjoying the slight movement as I hung suspended in the air. This time I didn't.

My eyes closed and I breathed to a count of four.

Josh taught me this meditative breathing, coaching me through more rigorous suspensions in the past.

Breathe in to a count of four. Hold for four. Then breathe out, once again counting to four.

I thought it silly the first time he talked me through it, but the more I did it, the more I enjoyed it.

My mind quieted with the slow intake of breath. The world faded as I took in an influx of energy inside my body. Held it and exchanged it with the spent, negative energy inside of me. Then I breathed it all out, releasing all the tension from my body and expelling negativity.

Through it all, peace swept through me.

Keeping my eyes closed helped. I could pretend I was anywhere. Oftentimes, the place I chose was that one night in my bed. The time when Josh snuck in to do nothing other than hold me in his arms. That was the first time I felt truly safe with him. It may have been the pivotal moment in our very unusual relationship.

Push and pull.

Those words defined everything about us.

The men on the couches having sex with the slaves were difficult to block out of my meditation. The sounds coming from that end of the room left little to the imagination.

The other man who had approached retreated to the couches. That made me feel a thousand times better because there was something repugnant about him which made my skin crawl.

Xavier shifted in front of me. He didn't repulse me like Carson. Instead, he reminded me of My Monster. The two of them shared similar qualities. A hard man, Xavier was dominant and unyielding. Nevertheless, I sensed compassion within him.

The same could not be said of Carson.

"Your Master will return in a moment." Xavier leaned close, speaking softly.

Deep in my meditation, I barely heard him, but then he kept his voice low, as if he were trying not to draw attention to us.

I said nothing. Josh told me to speak to no one and I would honor his wishes. Pleasing him brought a sense of fulfillment I was only now accepting as something I craved.

I did it not because it was expected. Not because he demanded it. And not because he forced it upon me. Although all of those reasons had once been powerful motivations in the past.

My reason for doing it now was because it was something I chose.

As if on cue, the doors to my left swung open. My eyes might be closed, but the depth of my meditative state accentuated my other senses, such as hearing.

Four people entered. One stumbled.

My eyelids ponderously lifted and my breathing shifted back to its normal pattern. The need to see My Monster, and reestablish our connection, pulled me from this floaty space.

But when my eyes opened. I blinked several times.

I saw My Monster, but there was something *different* about him.

Don't jump to conclusions.

A gorgeous woman stumbled between two men. Her hands had been manacled to a pole placed behind her head. The two men jerked her forward, nearly tripping her, as My Monster proudly walked in front of them.

The scowl in his face was one I knew well, except it was…different. The green depths of his eyes flickered with the same menacing ferocity I feared and respected, but didn't *feel* the same. His purposeful stride carried him past me, but it was as if he were a half beat behind.

I couldn't shake the feeling something was wrong.

What the hell is going on?

"You fucking prick!" the woman yelled.

The two men forced her ahead of them, toward the center of the room.

She kicked out at them, but her foot connected with nothing as the man to her left dodged to the side. She stumbled, and would have fallen, if not for the other man who gripped the metal pole and held her up.

"Gentlemen, welcome to this evening's main event." My Monster stopped in front of those gathered on the couches. He swept an arm back toward the woman. "Let me introduce Kate Summers."

Carson gave a low chuckle and shifted in his seat, eagerly propping his elbows on his knees. The others leaned back and pushed the women who'd been pleasuring them to the side.

"As you know, Kate orchestrated my arrest. I'm sure the cunt thought I'd be locked up for good, but the wonderful state of Georgia saw fit to release me."

Laughter sounded from the men.

"You deserve to rot behind bars," Kate screeched.

The two men who entered with My Monster attached her to the St. Andrews Cross. She kicked and hissed, fighting them with all her strength. Unfortunately, she was no match for the men.

Knowing the scene which had played out on that cross the last time I was in this room, my belly churned and bile rose in the back of my throat.

This can't be real?

Looks real

Don't jump to conclusions!

I tried listening to that voice in my head, but found that impossible. I had watched My Monster kill the girl with the spiky hair. He strangled the life out of her.

"My father died the night of my arrest." He stepped close to the woman and punched her in the stomach.

A loud whoosh escaped her mouth and she doubled over, or at least as far as she could with her arms tied over her head.

The two men worked to fasten her wrists to the cross. They removed the pole and bent to secure her ankles. She kicked free and clocked one of them in the jaw.

"Fucking bitch!" He worked his jaw side to side, then whipped his hand out to grab her ankle. With a tug, he yanked her foot to the side.

Her entire body dropped and she cried out as she fell, suspended only by the cuffs around her wrists. Quickly, he buckled her ankle to the bottom of the cross.

Working beside him, the other man did the same with her opposite leg. She was now spread eagle, legs apart, with her hands secured overhead. Her back was to me and I could no longer see her face.

"Tonight, Kate will pay; a life for a life." My Monster's voice filled with profound loss.

"You fucking monster. You won't get away with this. My Master will hunt you down. He'll kill you."

My Monster looked to his audience and his lip curled in a sneer. "My brother is a pansy-assed idiot. This time he'll be too late." Hatred spilled from his mouth with the mention of a brother. He turned to the woman and drew a kill line across his throat with his index finger.

Finally, it clicked.

This isn't your monster.

Josh has a twin.

It had to be because it explained how he looked, sounded, and acted like Josh. I felt sure of it.

Only, if that was the case, it generated more questions than it answered.

They weren't just identical. They were indistinguishable. How was that possible? I understood identical twins. Everyone knew about twins, but there were always subtle differences.

This man looked, and moved, exactly like My Monster.

He continued on, saying how Kate would suffer before paying the ultimate price. She twisted in her bonds, trying to free herself, but her efforts were futile.

The man who wasn't My Monster approached me. Our gazes locked. Tension lined his eyes and the muscles of his jaw bunched. He stopped in front of me, his gaze wandering over the intricate rope work with what looked like admiration.

Without saying a word, he continued to the wall behind me. I couldn't see what he did unless I swung myself around, but I didn't dare move. If I put myself in a spin, I wouldn't be able to keep my eye on the room, and there was no way in hell I would willingly put my back to those men.

Not-Josh walked past me. A bullwhip coiled in his grip and death stirred in the jade-green depths of his eyes. His fingers gripped the handle and he shook out the coils until they trailed behind him.

"I've been looking forward to this for a very long time. It's going to be my pleasure making you pay." His arm drew back then snapped forward. It sounded like a bullet went off, but it was only the cracking of the whip.

Kate screamed as he tore into her back, cutting through the fabric of her shirt and drawing blood.

He paced around her, muttering about his father, her crimes, how he would make her suffer. Every now and then, he struck her with the whip.

Each time, she screamed.

It didn't take long before her shirt was saturated with her blood. Tiny cuts crisscrossed the expanse of her back and her entire body shook. She hung from her wrists, sobbing, as his arm snapped forward and back.

Forward and back.

Tears spilled down my cheeks. I winced with each crack of the whip. But there was nothing I could do for the poor woman.

For the first time, I felt true fear. What was to keep him from turning that whip on me?

The two men who brought Kate into the room moved to stand on either side of me. I closed my eyes and wished them away. They responded by spreading their legs in a broad stance and crossing their hands lightly in front of themselves, like some modified form of parade rest. They said nothing as they bracketed me.

The whipping continued until only tatters of Kate's shirt remained. Soaked through, what had once been white was now blood red.

I cried for her as breath huffed in and out of the poor woman. Her legs shook as she struggled to stand, but each strike of the whip took the strength from her until she sagged in her bonds.

The men on the couches looked on with eager expressions plastered on their faces. Feral and depraved, they lapped up her screams and soaked in her misery.

Each crack of the whip brought smiles to their faces as Kate cried out in agony.

"This is what I have to offer," not-Josh said. "Pure, unadulterated pain. Your clients will watch behind the safety of privacy shields, or they can choose to participate and deal the killing blow. Depending on your clients tastes, rape can be a part of this. Not simulated rape with a willing slave who performs as the client demands. This is one-hundred percent real. And for an extra fee, they can designate who they want killed and we will make it happen."

"Impressive." The evil man rubbed his hands on his knees.

"Every event will be tailored to the client's demands. Rape. Torture. Maiming. Whatever floats their boat. And the pièce de résistance …"

The man clapped. "Bravo, but how will my clients be protected? Murder for pay is risky business."

"A man who runs death matches isn't concerned about legality. I'm certain you've figured that part out."

"You seem to know a lot about my business."

"We share common friends. My connections remain strong despite my incarceration and I've spent time reestablishing those relationships. And I'm looking forward to observing your operation."

"I see." Carson shifted back in his seat.

Not-Josh's arm drew back and a *crack* rent the air.

Kate Summers no longer screamed. A low groan escaped her ravaged body. The despair and defeat in that sound ripped me apart from the inside out. Josh told me not to speak, but he said nothing about blubbering sobs. My cries filled the room, overtaking the devastating ruin that was Kate Summers.

He gripped Kate's jaw. Lifting her head, he turned it roughly back and forth, then let go. Her chin dropped.

I didn't think she was conscious.

The glint of a knife flashed seconds before he slashed her neck. Blood spurted across his chest as his hand shot forward. He gripped her throat and his guttural voice echoed in the room.

"Last time, I held the cut across your neck to keep you from bleeding out. I'll do that for you now, but you won't die from that.

Your very last breath will be the one I choose." He tightened his grip.

Kate sagged in her bonds and a gurgle escaped as she tried to breathe. Her body convulsively jerked, then stilled a few seconds later.

Not-Josh snapped the fingers of his free hand and the men beside me jogged toward him.

"Get rid of her." He held her against the cross while the two men unbuckled her legs and then her wrists.

"Hang on a moment." The evil man placed two fingers alongside Kate's neck. After a few seconds, he gave a sharp nod. "Dead as a doornail. Well done, and might I say intoxicating." He took in a deep breath. "I can definitely see more participants than observers."

Not-Josh lifted Kate's body off the cross and threw her into the arms of one of the guards. "Take out the trash."

Her body hung limply over the guard's shoulder as he headed toward the exit.

Not-Josh turned to me then made a point of looking back toward the couches. He clapped his hands, a sharp retort, which had me jerking in the rope.

"Music. Slaves. And more fucking. Whatever your heart desires."

A shrill sound filled the room. The evil man pulled out his cellphone from his breast pocket and lifted it to his ear. He cocked his head, listening to whomever was on the other line. Then he looked to Not-Josh.

"My partner is interested in pursuing this further."

"We can discuss business in a bit." Not-Josh wiped the sweat from his brow. "I need to get the bitch's blood off of me."

Without another word, or glance toward me, he marched out of the room. The other guard returned to stand by my side and resumed his modified parade rest.

My insides twisted in knots and I thought I was going to get sick.

Don't jump to conclusions.

I know!

But how could I forget what I had just seen? And heard?

Chapter 4

Josh

"You're going to wear a hole in the carpet." Mitzy looked at me, making an exaggerated eye roll. It seemed to be an expression Kate's perky assistant had mastered.

Everything she did was like that: over the top, larger than life, greater, better, or worse than it really was.

"You have major trust issues," she continued with her flippant monologue, telling me everything I was doing wrong.

She didn't know the half of my issues surrounding trust. There was no one, literally, in this world who I trusted.

"Trust?" I glared at her. "Is that what you think this is?"

Clara was in the other room, helpless and suspended in front of monsters, and Mitzy was giving me grief about wearing a hole in the carpet? The girl had no idea the restraint I displayed while Jake was in there instead of me.

"Stop pacing and take a deep breath," Mitzy said. "Everything is going as planned."

I pointed to the video feed of the other room and tried to keep my voice level.

My brother laid into Kate with a fury I never expected.

"How can you sit there and watch that?"

"I'm not watching. And what does it matter? Kate's the Mistress of Pain. She didn't earn that name for nothing."

"It's brutal."

Mitzy shrugged. "It's what they do. I don't judge. You shouldn't either."

I was no stranger to sadism. For most of my life, I considered myself a hard-core sadist, at least until I met Clara. She turned everything I knew on its head.

I still craved control. There would be no denying my basic makeup, but there were many ways to dominate without inflicting pain.

Clara taught me this. She showed me how the connection we forged could be more powerful than any of the rest. I didn't need to hurt her to obtain gratification. Hell, all I had to do was be in the same room with my sweet Clara. With her beside me, I could do anything. Be anything. Most importantly, she made me want to be the kind of man she could love.

Kate and Jake took masochism and sadism to the extreme. We'd talked about making our little production realistic, but not with that degree of brutality.

Mistress of Pain?

I severely underestimated Kate Summers.

"I'm not judging." I pulled at the roots of my hair with frustration because that was exactly what I had done. "I didn't expect it to be that brutal."

"They're doing great. It's totally believable, and it's magnificent."

"It's disgusting."

"Coming from you that's kind of funny." She cocked her head. "Something's different about you." Mitzy propped her tiny fists on her slender hips. "You're almost human."

"Almost human?"

"Yeah, you know, like a living, breathing, compassionate human being. You've lost your disgusting edge."

"Is that so?" I had to suffer through another exaggerated eye roll before she answered.

"Yeah, you're not a psychopath after all. Who knew?" She pointed to the video feed. "After the things you did, I'm surprised any of that bothers you."

It did.

Every bit of it turned my stomach and put a sour taste in my mouth.

"I'm surprised it doesn't bother you," I said, countering.

Mitzy shrugged. "It's no worse than watching a horror movie. Compared to the things you've done, this is tame."

Her continued reference to my past crimes had the fine hairs at the back of my neck lifting. Those were things I didn't want to remember, and I certainly didn't need this slip of a girl reminding me of the monstrous things I'd done. I knew what I'd done.

And I most certainly didn't need to relive it. Shit, my hands were shaking. I put my palm to my face and dragged it down to my jaw. I'd been the worst human being.

Honestly, I hadn't expected to react this strongly to what was happening in the other room. Flashbacks haunted me. Images of Kate and Lily strung up from beams in that abandoned warehouse.

Lily's screams.

The flash of a knife.

Blood.

There'd been so much blood.

"I served my time." I barely kept my voice from shaking. Shit, I needed to sit down. I needed to stop watching the feed from the other room.

"No, you didn't." Her eyelids fluttered and she looked at me as if I was an idiot.

"I have the parole papers to prove it." I didn't know why I felt a need to defend myself, but I did.

"That doesn't change what you did." She crossed her arms and hitched a hip on the counter. Her steady stare told me exactly what she thought of me.

"We're not having this conversation. I don't have to prove myself to you, or anyone." I didn't have time for this shit, and hell if I cared what she thought about me.

Except you do care.

Shut up.

In the other room, my brother rained devastation down on Kate. She sagged in her bonds and appeared to be unconscious. Jake stopped whipping her and moved around to the front of the cross. It wouldn't be long now before he dealt the final blow.

"You'd still be in jail if it weren't for Kate," Mitzy continued the pointless conversation.

I spun around. "She had nothing to do with my release."

"You're not that stupid. At least Jake isn't so thickheaded. How do you think a serial rapist received a commuted sentence? You think that just happened?"

I assumed exactly that.

Overcrowding in the penal system resulted in many criminals serving abbreviated sentences. Although, I now was beginning to think other forces had been at play.

All of this had been my plan, but in reality, it had been orchestrated by Kate, Mitzy, and Lily long before I found myself in that parking lot outside the prison.

They planned every detail from my early release to acquiring Clara at the auction. I adjusted their plan, tweaking it to ensure success, but at the center of it all, Kate, Mitzy, and Lily choreographed this insanity.

I wasn't sure how I felt about that.

The whole operation made me feel like I was covered in filth. That wasn't the kind of man I wanted to become and Mitzy thought I was a psychopath. Would I never escape the demons of my past?

I'd been brainwashed by my father and forced to do unspeakable things because of *the crazy* infesting his mind, but I wasn't evil. Not that I tried to justify my actions, but damn if I didn't feel victimized by the whole thing.

My life could have been different.

So many choices led me down the wrong path. What I wouldn't give to go back and chose left instead of right. I shook my head. Wishing and wanting were useless things. The only person responsible for my life was me, and it was past time to own up to it all.

Mitzy knew nothing about the kind of man I could be, and I wouldn't let her define me.

"What we're doing will save lives." Mitzy gestured to the live video feed. "Here we go. Get ready."

Jake slit Kate's throat and strangled her in front of a room of real psychopaths, sociopaths, and villainous men. They were the true monsters.

Not me.

Damnit all.

Not me!

We had a couple minutes before Jake and I swapped out. On screen, Kate's death played out.

"Save?" I stalked away from Kate's friend. "What about the girls we didn't save? The ones from the auction who are living in hell? We didn't save them."

Mitzy gave another dramatic eye roll. "You think we let those men take those girls?"

"What are you saying?" I stopped in my tracks.

"You really are a fool," she said with a snort. "We didn't abandon those girls. Men are so dense." Her derisive snort pierced the air.

I rushed her, gripped her throat, and held her against the wall. Her toes dangled a few inches above the floor and her heels kicked against the baseboards while the whites of her eyes showed.

"What are you saying?"

She clutched at my hand, trying to peel my fingers away from her throat. My grip tightened. Her face turned blue, deepened to purple, and the capillaries of her cheeks burst.

The door behind us banged open.

"Oh my God!" Xavier's slave, Raven, raced into the room. A fiery ball of fury, she attacked me with her tiny fists. "Let her go!" She tried to peel my fingers from around Mitzy's throat.

I released Mitzy and she dropped to the floor where she clutched at her throat and gasped.

"What the fuck are you talking about?" My words came out in a guttural roar. "If you rescued those girls, you placed us all in danger. You put Clara in danger. That's not something you can hide, and you can bet Carson investigated all those buyers. He looked into them, their pasts, and likely what they're doing with their new acquisitions right now. You've jeopardized everything!"

Mitzy gripped her throat, gagging and coughing, as she looked at me with murder in her eyes.

I stepped close, invading her space, fists clenched tight as Raven punched me in the gut. Her small frame held zero power and I batted her away like a gnat.

"I'm fucking serious." I pressed Mitzy to explain. "You've ruined this operation."

"You really are a bastard, you know that?" Mitzy rubbed at her throat.

"And you're a fucking bitch. Tell me what you meant."

"Fine!" Mitzy's voice croaked and she worked to swallow against the swelling in her throat. "Did you really think we'd do nothing for those girls and just send them off to be raped?"

"That's exactly what I thought." It's what they said would happen.

My job was to buy a girl and make her mine.

I bought Clara and trained her to be a perfect slave. All those other girls were collateral damage, consigned to their fates as hapless victims I couldn't save.

I accepted that.

I moved on.

Clara was all that mattered.

And Wu's kids.

Girls forced into sexual slavery.

And boys forced to fight to the death.

They mattered too, and I did all of this for them. Those other girls who shared the stage with Clara? I left them to their fates and forgot them.

Maybe I was a monster.

"You better start talking now." My fingers curled into fists and I had to work hard to relax. If I didn't, I was going to seriously injure Mitzy and Raven.

It was just the three of us in this room. Jake and Kate were on stage. Skye, Tia, and Ryker waited in the wings to revive Kate after her death. Bay and Chad were the muscle. Chambers and Abrams pretended to be buyers and potential clients. And Xavier played the role of dutiful host. I could kill Mitzy and Raven if that's what I chose and no one could stop me.

It was a miracle they both still breathed.

Raven looked between Mitzy and I as she pieced together our conversation. "Josh, you need to calm down. It's not what you think. Forest managed the auction." She kept her voice calm, trying to ease the tension in the room. "Those girls are safe. No one's cover has been blown."

"And no one thought to clue me in on that part of the plan?" Fury bloomed within me, and I let out my anger with my fist. I punched the wall. Mitzy and Raven jumped, and I shook out my hand.

Forest had no right. He hid behind a computer screen manipulating events from the safety of anonymity. I had yet to meet the man in person and didn't understand his paranoia. I'd written him off as a useless tech asset, but wondered how much of this whole thing had been orchestrated by him.

Not that it mattered. This wasn't the kind of battle fought behind the safety of a computer. It was the kind fought with fists. It was dirty. Bloody. And people would die.

From what I'd seen, Forest wasn't the kind of man who understood what it took to deal with the men in that other room. He might look formidable on the screen, but I sensed he was a twatwaffle.

While I hated to admit it, Raven had a point. I needed to focus and get my head back in the game.

Right now, that meant waiting in the room I had dubbed Command and Control.

Only none of us were in command.

And none of us controlled anything.

All of that belonged to the players on stage.

In that room, Carson rose from the couch and pressed his fingers against Kate's throat. Bile rose in mine. If he touched Clara, there was no way I wouldn't remove his hand from his body. Hell, I'd take his entire arm. That Jake stood there and allowed Carson to touch his girl had me granting him extreme respect.

I wouldn't have that degree of self-control.

But I sensed he and Kate had discussed every permutation of this scene. The trust they shared rivaled anything I hoped to ever share with another human. My respect wasn't healthy. It was profound.

Once again, I wished for a tenth of what my brother shared with Kate.

Which reminded me how helpless Clara remained. I itched to return to her.

To protect her.

To shelter her.

To love her.

Bay was on the move. Called over by Jake, Kate was cut from the St. Andrews Cross and carried from the room. She would be taken to an adjacent room where the medical team waited. Jake stayed behind for a moment before excusing himself to clean up.

"We're not done with this conversation." I had to meet Jake and exchange clothes.

As I stalked out into the hall I decided I was through being manipulated and used. From here on out, things would be done my way, which meant I would tell Clara everything.

Jake met me in the hall. His gaze darted toward the room where Bay had taken Kate. I yanked off my T-shirt and stepped out of my jeans. Jake mirrored my motions, stripping in the hall while we passed clothing between us.

Kate's blood spattered across his cheek and was on the shirt. I was *washing it off*, but would keep the bloodied shirt. He tossed his pants to me, and didn't bother to dress. Without a word, he rushed into the room where Skye, Tia, and Ryker huddled around Kate's body.

Their movements were practiced, sure, and completely devoid of emotion. I took a second to poke my head in.

Skye held her finger against Kate's neck. Ryker stood at the head of the bed. He held a face mask over Kate's nose and mouth and pumped a large bag connected to it, breathing for Kate, while Tia inserted a needle into Kate's arm. She administered something from a syringe.

"I have a pulse." Skye said. "Is she breathing on her own?"

Ryker paused in his bagging and all three of them stared at Kate's chest. My brother hovered a few feet back, anxiously shifting from foot to foot. If I'd been him, I didn't think I'd be able to stand there like that. I'd be right by Clara's side, probably getting in the way and making things worse.

Kate took a breath, and I think we all released ours. I hadn't realized I'd been holding mine, but I needed to know Kate was safe.

There was nothing I could do in there, and my brother certainly didn't need my support. The bastard still wasn't speaking to me. Perhaps he never would.

I put on my game face and turned back down the hall. It was time to seal the deal and begin the next phase of the operation.

Chapter 5

Clara

How do I explain this floaty feeling? My Monster wrapped me in his embrace of silk and rope. In this cocoon, nothing could touch me. In this space, I was safe.

I was loved.

I felt secure that all was well in my world as I hung in a contraption of rope. My very existence depended upon the good will of monstrous men, and yet I found myself without fear. Something greater than myself was at play. I felt it.

I believed it.

Josh wasn't evil.

Everything here had been staged. Which meant…that woman didn't die. And the one with spiky hair hadn't either. This was what he was trying to tell me with his coded message.

I wanted to sing it to the world.

One of the side doors banged open, the same door through which Not-Josh had stormed out saying he needed to clean up.

I peeked, afraid of what I would see, and quickly slammed my eyes closed at the rage in his face. Tension girded his frame, bunching in his muscles as he closed the distance, making a beeline for me.

"That was an impressive show." Carson clapped. The expression on his face didn't match the clapping. It felt forced. The man hid his vileness well. "We're in."

"We?" Josh pulled up short. "I didn't realize there was a we involved."

"My business partner. While you were gone, we discussed how this might fit into our business. We'd like to extend you an invitation to see our operation and see how we can fold the two of them together."

"Our client list is generally not this extreme." Abrams shifted his attention to Chambers. "What do you think?"

"We should discuss particulars," Chambers said, "before withdrawing our interest."

I flexed my muscles while the men talked, which put me into a slight rocking motion. Josh noticed and locked eyes with me. The tiniest shake of his head told me to stop. I supposed he didn't want me drawing attention to myself. I stilled and practiced the breathing exercises he taught me. Hopefully, this whole evening would end soon.

"The particulars are easy. I provide the victims and venue. You bring the clients. I take twenty percent and you keep the rest."

"Only twenty?" Carson sounded surprised. "I expected a larger cut."

"You're not my only client."

"I'm not comfortable being one of many. It exposes us to unnecessary risk." Carson approached the center of the room. He turned to Chambers and Abrams. "Actually, we're interested in exclusivity."

"Exclusivity can be yours for fifty percent." Josh approached me and placed a hand on my knee, stilling my slight swaying. His fingers dug in, not to hurt, but more to ground himself.

"I can definitely see the possibilities." Carson gave a low chuckle and turned to the one man in the room who had said virtually nothing. "Xavier, you have the most interesting friends. What are your thoughts on this?"

"There's opportunity here." Xavier lifted a snifter of brandy. "I sense growth potential."

"What's your interest?"

"Now that is private business between myself and Mr. Davenport."

"You two are in business together then?"

"Of course. Why does that come as a surprise?"

"No surprise, just didn't think you would get your hands dirty. That's not like you."

"You'd be surprised at the things I'm involved in."

Josh left me to join the men at the couches. While they talked business, I rocked in the rope. The slaves were brought back. There was more sloppy sex.

Then, finally, the evening came to an end. Josh and Carson shook hands. Chambers and Abrams excused themselves. Xavier led everyone out, leaving me and Josh alone.

He came over and placed his hands on me.

"You did well. How are you feeling?" He reached overhead to release the rope.

"Good." That had been the longest I'd been held in suspension. Surprisingly, my joints felt great and there were no issues with circulation.

"We need to talk." He began the arduous task of untying the knots. I opened my mouth to speak, but he placed his finger over my lips. With a sharp shake of his head, he said, "Later."

Before I could say anything, he leaned forward and kissed me.

Soft and hesitant, he was reverent, as if asking permission. I would have thrown my arms around his neck if I could, but they were still tied up.

Didn't he know he no longer needed permission to kiss me?

I had given him my heart when I gave him my body. In every way, I belonged to him.

As the ropes fell away, an awkwardness grew between us. His movements became more hesitant and unsure, stilted even. He refused to look me in the eye. Once I was free, he extended his hand and lifted me to my feet. After I found my balance, he released my hand.

I wobbled without his strength to support me and wrapped my

arms around my nakedness feeling suddenly shy.

"Follow me."

I assumed we were still in Master and slave mode, so I crossed my hands in front of me and made myself meek.

"Yes, Sir."

His shoulders hitched, but he said nothing as he led me out of that horrible place.

I thought he would take me back to my cell. I hoped he might bring me to the room he was staying in. The thought of exploring a real bed with him made my body ache in the most delicious way. What I did not expect was for him to wrap a robe around me and take me outside.

He led me through a beautiful garden and to a cove with bleach-white sand kissing mirror-smooth waters. A deep-blue dome capped the sky and wispy clouds floated far overhead. The sun rained sunshine down on me, warming my skin, as a gentle breeze rolled inward from the sea.

"We can talk out here," he said. "No cameras."

"It's beautiful." I wanted to ask what we needed to talk about, but deflected because I sensed he needed a moment to gather his thoughts.

Instead of standing beside me, he placed distance between us. His hands went to his head where he dug his fingers into his hair and tugged at the roots. I was beginning to recognize what that meant and felt the need to go to him.

The light breeze lifted my hair and blew it around. It gusted open my robe, exposing my toned legs to the sun. After too many days trapped indoors, the sunlight felt amazing on my skin.

He dropped his hands to his sides and gestured to the pristine beach and welcoming waters. "You deserve beautiful things. You deserve to be pampered and loved." His lips pressed together. "I'm letting you go."

"Letting me go?" I cocked my head.

"You're free." He gave a sharp nod and took two steps back.

"Just like that?" I squinted into the sun. "I'm free?"

"Well, not exactly free. You won't be able to go back to your previous life. I'm sorry for that, but it's unavoidable. You'll be placed in witness protection. Given a new identity. You'll have a chance to start a new life. But, you're free from this."

"This?" I couldn't believe my ears. "Do you mean us?"

"What I did to you is something I regret, and I'm sorry for it. I won't ask your forgiveness. I don't deserve it, except to say it was necessary. I don't expect you to understand, but I did my best to not make it a living nightmare."

"Necessary?" I glanced back toward the thick foliage which hid the expansive estate from view. "You didn't bring me out here, where there are no cameras, to tell me I'm free." My fingers curled into tight little fists. "Don't wimp out on me, Josh. Not now."

That stirred a reaction. He took one step toward me, *My Monster* coming to correct, but then he pulled up short and the monster retreated.

"What do you mean wimp out on you?"

"What happened back there—"

"Was vile, and I'm sorry you had to see it." He bent his head. "It was fake. I want you to know that."

"No shit, Sherlock." I snapped.

His head shot up and a dangerous glint simmered in his eyes. He didn't like when I talked back to him, but he did nothing.

My Monster, however, had disappeared, leaving only a man standing in front of me. It might be crazy, but I missed the monster and the imbalance of our power which had been the only constant in my life these past few weeks.

"I'm not talking about the fake deaths. I knew the moment your twin walked in."

"Wait, you knew that wasn't me?" His mouth gaped.

"I know everything about you, every nuance. Hell, I could sense you before you ever unlocked my door. I know how you smell, how you breathe, how you walk…and that wasn't you. How can you want to free me after what happened back there?"

"How could I not? That world back there?" He pointed back toward the estate. "It's vile, filthy, and disgusting. I don't want you anywhere near it."

"But what about me?"

"Ah…" He gave a nod. "You're talking about the sex."

"Fuck you!" My anger burst outward in full force. He was not going to get away with tossing me out that easily.

"Watch your language."

"Or what? You'll put me over your knee? Spank me until I cry? You freed me. You don't have that power anymore."

"I said to watch your language…" He spoke slowly, making sure I understood, "because it turns me on when you disobey me." He pointed to the tenting in his pants. "My self-control is stretched to its limit, Clara. Keep it up and that's exactly where you'll land; over my knee until you scream, then I'll make you ride my cock."

"You make it sound so romantic."

"It's just sex."

"It wasn't just sex, and you know it. If it was, we wouldn't be out here right now arguing about whether I'll let you free me."

"We're not arguing about that. You're free. End of story."

"You take me, make me yours, then walk away when you're done with me?" I didn't believe a word he said. "You don't get to take the easy way out of this…Josh." Maybe if I said his name, he'd realize we were talking about something much more important than my freedom.

"You don't want what I have to offer…Clara." He threw my name back at me. "Your mind is twisted and confused. What you feel for me, or think you feel, it's not real. It's the product of what I did."

"I'm fully aware of what you did to me." I was two seconds from storming off in a huff, and I probably would have if he hadn't said what he did about spanking me and making me ride his cock. As filthy as that sounded, the aching throb between my legs didn't lie.

That shit turned me on.

Maybe I was fucked in the head? Maybe I didn't care?

"I also know what happened back there wasn't just sex. You can deny it all you want, but you made love to me. Everything you did to me, out of all the things you did, not once did you force yourself on me."

"That doesn't excuse what I did."

"I'm not excusing anything. It was wrong. Everything about it was wrong, but I forgave you. Shit, I forgive you now, just don't throw me away."

"Is that what you think? I'm throwing you away?"

"You literally just told me I would be placed in witness protection and given a new identity. If that's not getting rid of me, I don't know what is."

"You can't go back to your old life, and you can't stay here. It's not safe."

"It's not safe because of whatever I witnessed back there, but the cat's out of the bag with that one."

"Then we're in agreement."

"The only thing we're in agreement about is the spanking you want to give me and riding your cock."

He covered his mouth, but couldn't hide the grin tugging at the corners of his lips.

"Don't tease me, Clara." His pupils dilated and he took a step toward me.

I took a step back and he stopped with a groan.

"I'm serious. You don't want to tease me."

"I'm not, but," I put up a hand to keep him in place, needing answers first, "you brought me here to tell me something you couldn't say in that house. Tell me everything. Don't leave me in the dark."

"You don't want to know."

"I do."

"There's nothing light and fluffy about what I have to say. It's all darkness, my sweet Clara."

"Have a little faith in me, *My Monster.* Trust that I won't break or fall apart. Trust that I won't run from you."

"You will after I tell you. You'll run and you won't ever look back."

"Are you so certain about that?" He didn't know me very well. I'd seen his worst, but I embraced his best.

"Positive."

Chapter 6

Josh

I ground my teeth together, then gestured to a spot on the sand beside me. Practically collapsing to the ground, I tugged at my shoes and pulled off my socks. While I dug my toes into the sand, Clara took a seat beside me.

"I'm a killer." It wasn't the best way to begin, but it was the truth.

"I know. Remember, you saved me from the men who tried to rape me."

"You've only seen what I became. You don't know what I am."

"Then tell me." She reached for my hand, but I jerked it away.

With a deep breath in, I took a minute to decide how to begin. "I've always been sexually dominant. I can't think of a single sexual encounter where I didn't take charge. My brother is the same, as is our best friend, Kevin. You could say we grew into it together."

"It?"

"BDSM. Bondage. Discipline, Sadism and Masochism. Your submission. My dominance…My love of bondage…" I turned to her. "These are parts of me I can't live without."

Her cheeks flushed and she looked away.

Yeah, I didn't think she understood how deeply ingrained it was in my psyche.

Even after spending weeks beneath my rule, the depths of my needs were incompatible with hers.

She wasn't a masochist, although deeply submissive. That's what I feared the most. Her submissive tendencies would lead her to accepting things she wasn't mentally prepared to handle.

"I crave control. It's not a game to me, and dispensing pain—"

"Turns you on. I know this."

"Knowing is one thing. Accepting it is another. Embracing it?" *Loving me?* "Well, that's something altogether different." I shifted on my butt. Just the thought of spanking her had me rock hard.

"I don't understand everything that's happened…"

"I'm getting to it. Just give me a moment to explain. It's complicated."

"No, that's not what I mean, and yes, I want you to tell me, but I was talking about me."

"What about you?"

"The pain…it's not something I ever thought…" She ducked her head, struggling to get her words out.

"You don't have to talk about it."

Her head snapped up. "I do if we're going to be together."

Together? Was that even an option?

"I don't think you understand. I'm letting you go."

"I'm choosing to stay."

"No."

That wasn't an option. It was too dangerous, especially as I moved into the next phase of this operation. I'd secured an invite to one of the death matches. No way in hell would I subject Clara to that. Boys would die, and I would have to let it happen.

Like the auction where I bought Clara, some would die for others to live. I didn't have to like it, but I understood the greater good. She wouldn't be touched by that evil. I wouldn't allow it.

"You can't tell me no," she said. "You don't get to make that choice for me."

"I can, and I will."

She dug her fingers into the sand and lifted a handful in her palm. Slowly, she let the grains of sand run out between her fingers.

"You took that choice from me the night of the auction. From that moment forward, I had no choice in anything. You said you're letting me go. Do you mean that?"

"Absolutely. You're free to go. Wherever you want. We'll set you up with a new identity, enough money you'll never want for anything. You'll have a good life."

"Then I choose you."

"Absolutely not."

"Why? You don't get to take this choice from me."

"You don't know what you're saying, and you haven't let me explain what's going on. It's too dangerous."

"I want to hear what you have to say, but I want you to listen to what I have to say first. I won't be your slave. I can't. I can't lose that much control over my life again. But, I remember what you said about if we had met another way. You were right."

I struggled to remember that conversation, then it hit me.

"Clara, forget about that. You'll find someone else."

"I never would have let you do the things you did to me if we'd met any other way. I would have seen it as abusive."

"It *was* abusive. Clara, the things I did were abusive."

"They were wrong. I'm not saying they weren't, but they changed me. I know it's crazy, and it makes no sense that I would like it, but it wasn't all bad. You were cruel, but you were also kind. You never hurt me more than I could handle, and you never took advantage of me. Don't you see?"

"I never would have done any of it, if it hadn't been for—"

"You don't understand. What I'm saying is that I never would have let you do those things to me, but if you hadn't, then *I* would never have known how much I liked it." She put her finger against her chin. "Like is the wrong word. It's not that I *liked it* as much as it felt like a part of me woke up. I didn't know what had been missing. I don't like when you hurt me, but I love when you take control." She squirmed, then turned to look directly at me. "I don't like your punishments, but they turn me on. Not the pain. I don't like that, it's something else."

My dick was so hard it was drilling a hole in my pants. This woman had no idea what she was doing to me by admitting her submission. I groaned and didn't try to hide as I adjusted my erection.

"If you don't stop, I'm going to fuck you right here."

She glanced around. "I've never had sex on the beach."

"You don't know what you're offering."

"I know exactly what I'm offering. And it's not easy to admit it, especially to you. It puts me in an awkward position."

"How's that?"

"Because now you know."

"Love, I've always known. You're a natural submissive, but offering yourself to me like this, it pushes buttons you don't want pushed. I can't separate pain and sex. They're one and the same to me."

"I'm okay with that."

"I'm a rapist." I don't know why I blurted it out like that, but the words spilled out. She needed to understand what I truly was and she needed to run before I lost the strength to let her go.

"No, you're not. You were very careful with me. You never—"

"I served five years of a twelve-year sentence for multiple counts of rape. You want to know the kind of man you're handing your submission to? I raped women to frame my twin brother for murder. I killed a girl in a scene where I lost control. I was incarcerated for two years in a jail in Thailand for murder and served five years in the United States Penitentiary, Atlanta for multiple counts of rape. That's the kind of man you're giving yourself to. I'm a monster. A real one."

I didn't understand the upwelling of anger inside of me, but I began to shout.

"I don't know how you've twisted me in your head into some kind of hero, but I'm not the good guy in this story. I'm a rapist, a murder, a man who traffics in sex slaves, and I've just entered into business with a man who kills boys for sport in an underground fight club while I hammer out the details of a snuff operation. I'm worse than a monster. I'm a living nightmare."

Her eyes widened as my words sunk in. Slowly, she rose to her feet.

I breathed out a sigh of relief. Finally, she would do the logical thing and run away as far as possible.

But she didn't. She stepped in front of me and gripped the edges of her robe. Slowly, she let the fabric fall from her shoulders. It slipped down to her waist, revealing her glorious tits, then slid off her hips and down to the sand. Standing naked before me, there was no fear in her eyes.

"You are a monster, but you're *My Monster*. Men do terrible things all the time, but you're living proof redemption can be found. I've said it before, and I'll say it again. I'll say it as many times as necessary. I. Forgive. You."

"Don't."

"I forgive you." She knelt before me and placed her palms on her knees. "Sometimes it takes a monster to bring down monstrous men. Who would go after them if not you?"

"No one."

"Exactly. You're saving innocents from death and fates worse than death. You may not be the typical hero, but you're not a monster."

"It's too dangerous for you to stay."

"I deserve to decide that for myself. Please don't force me to leave. Given a choice, I choose you."

"If I make it out of this alive, and there's a possibility I won't, I don't know if I can live without—"

She placed her hand on mine and lifted it to her lips. "I can't live without it either. Now that I know how it feels, how you make me feel, my life will never be the same. You've had a lot longer to figure out what you need. Give me some time to discover what I need."

I pulled her into my lap, but she twisted in my grip to straddle my hips. Her naked pussy heated the fabric of my pants and my dick took notice.

"You're driving me insane."

"I've never had sex on the beach, but from the looks of this sand we'll need to be careful. What do you say, *Monster?* Wanna make love to your girl?"

My girl? That sounded so much better than *my slave.* I loved the possessiveness and her willingness.

"Fuck yeah." I gripped her hips and ground her hot pussy over my crotch. My dick twitched with the need to be free. Fortunately, I didn't need to wait long.

Clara reached between us. A quick flick of her thumb and my pants button was undone. She gripped the metal of my zipper and unzipped me. Her delicate hand reached in and freed my hungry cock.

I about came right then.

She wrapped her arms around my neck and brushed her lips over my hard jaw. "I'm yours. You're not going to scare me away, and whatever you have to face, we face it together. All I see is you. Your past doesn't define you. What you choose to do with your future does. You're a man willing to sacrifice himself to save others. That makes you a hero in my book."

Her sweet lips trailed a path of utter destruction to my ear where she whispered soft and delicately. "You won't break me."

"You're killing me, sweet Clara. I'm going to come like a one-pump-and-done virgin if you're not careful."

She stroked me from root to tip. "You mean like this?"

My eyes about rolled into the back of my head with the pleasure coursing through my body. I wanted to sheath myself in her wet heat, but I allowed her to take the lead.

"If you tease me, I'll paddle your ass."

"Mmm, that makes me wet."

I reached between us and pressed my fingers against her folds.

"You're fucking drenched and ready for me."

"That's what you do to me." She kissed my ear. Her body stilled. "Take me."

It was all the encouragement I needed. I caught the back of her neck and crushed my mouth to hers. I kissed her hard, with a bruising aggression meant to dominate and lay claim to what was mine. She might be on top, but I was in charge. I needed her to prove to me that she could handle it, that she willingly surrendered control.

I demanded entrance to her mouth, and she parted for me. My tongue slipped inside, demanding, seeking, tasting and claiming. Meanwhile, I peeled her hand off my cock and angled it to thrust inside her pussy. It was all I could do to resist jerking my hips upward and ramming into her, but I wanted her to make the first move. I needed her to take that step. I needed it because I had to prove I was not in fact a monster, and that she willingly gave this to me.

Her fingers dug into the back of my neck and her tiny gasps sent shivers of electricity shooting through my body. The energy gathered in my groin and sparked an unrelenting need to thrust and rut.

The defined length of my erection jutted between her legs and lined up for the plunge.

I tore my mouth from hers and stared deep into her eyes. "If you want it, take it. There won't be many opportunities where you're in control."

"Do you promise?" She bit her lip, and I understood. Her taking control now was important to us both. It reset the dynamic between us, one where I didn't take and where she gave willingly.

My fingers gripped her hips, digging in where they would most definitely leave a bruise. She didn't seem to notice the pain, leaving me to wonder how much of that would be in our future.

Her body trembled over mine as she hovered over the tip of my cock.

"It's okay," I said, "go as slow as you need."

If she could see what I saw, how her body responded to my commands, then she would understand how frighteningly beautiful she could be. For the first time, I felt real fear. That trust would break me if I ever failed her.

She needed this moment as much, or more, than I did because she needed to be in control for once, and yet still subject to my will. Her lips pressed tight as she considered how to proceed.

"I've never done this before. I've never straddled a man."

"You can go slow, or fast. I'm here with you." My fingers curled into the skin over her hips.

"I need help."

"Do you trust me?"

She gave a nod. The tension in her body melted away the moment I took over. Her breathing pulled in erratic jerks as I gripped her hips and pulled her down on me while simultaneously thrusting upward. I didn't think I'd last if this happened slow.

Once I buried myself in her sweet heat, I held her there, allowing her to accommodate to my girth and breathe against any pain that may have caused. But I worried for no reason. Her eyes flew open and she gave a gasp of pleasure. Her hips pulled back, then rocked forward.

"Oh my God, it feels..."

Like the most amazing thing on the planet.

Our bodies fit together like a glove, molded to every curve as her hips took up a rhythm. The warm caress of her lips against mine drove every thought out of my head except one.

I needed this woman in my life.

The heat of her pussy drove me insane. Warm, sensual undulations of her body rocked against mine and it was all I could do to hold on and not rush through our union. I kissed her breast, sucking in her nipple as she rocked her hips faster. Playing with her nipple, I tortured it with flicks of my tongue and nips from my teeth, combining pleasure and pain into one overwhelming sensation. She pressed her chest forward, pushing her breast against my mouth as her gasps turned into low, throaty moans.

She moved over me, arching her back as she gyrated over my cock.

"Josh..." My name fell like a plea from her mouth, a secret gift delivered from her mouth to mine.

She rose against me, finding her rhythm, and we shared an ebb and flow of sensation. Heat pooled between us. Our lips met and the kiss deepened. My hands on her body tightened as her grip around my neck intensified.

Somewhere in there, we lost our rhythm as our kiss became

needy and her movements became frantic. My control began to slip, but I forced myself to rein in the beast. This was Clara, not my slave, but rather my girl.

We could only move forward if I proved I could handle this. Her hips jerked and she gasped.

"Harder," she said with a moan.

I took over with a jerk of my hips and thrust like I could somehow bury my cock inside her forever. In truth, I'd found my way home. My heart swelled as I found my rhythm, overtaking the one she set. Clara groaned as she held on and let pleasure rush through her body.

I pressed my lips against the shallow dip of her shoulder and let my tongue trace to the wing of her collar bone. That put me at the base of her neck and I sucked at the soft tissues there. She would have a hickey there for the next few days that would be impossible to hide.

My hips stabbed upward, no longer with coordinated thrusts. I sought our pleasure, driving us up an explosive cliff. Her legs wrapped around my hips and her body welcomed every thrust as we spiraled ever upward.

My body shook as all restraint fled me. There was only one outcome left. I held off until her orgasm slammed into her with a whole-body shudder, trembling and groaning with desperate pleasure. The walls of her pussy rippled along the length of my cock, demanding that I follow her into the abyss.

In this, I obeyed her command and released the last of my restraint. Pleasure coursed through me as I came inside of her with a throaty roar.

Mine!

The beast within me snapped and agreed. Clara belonged to me now because there was no way I would ever let her go.

"I love you." She collapsed against me, spent and satisfied.

"I love you more." Even if I didn't deserve it, but that no longer mattered. It wasn't for me to say what I did and didn't deserve. She had forgiven me, and maybe, someday, I would learn to forgive myself. Until then, I would accept the forgiveness she freely gave.

Chapter 7

Clara

Josh and I spent the next few hours on the beach. We splashed in the water, playing like children, then ventured out deeper into the cove, matching each other stroke for stroke, as we glided across an amazing coral reef. When we tired, we returned to the beach and built our fortresses. He built a castle. I build a fort.

Then we took turns lobbing sand at our creations until his castle walls fell. The tide came in and we made love again. Sex on the beach sounds more romantic in theory than practice and we had to abort our second attempt of making love as the low waves rolled into shore. He carried me waist deep and we washed away all the sand which clung to our skin.

With my legs wrapped around his hips, we came together with a new understanding of how our future might look. I would always be his and he would always be mine, but he was no longer my Master.

"You're getting a sunburn," he announced, which ended our foray on the beach. Retreating back to the mansion, we showered together for the first time.

A yawn escaped me while I knelt before him to take him into my mouth which made him laugh.

He scooped me up into his arms. "You can't suck a man's cock and yawn while doing it."

"I'm sorry," I said as another yawn escaped me. "It's not personal. I'm just a little tired. It's been a big day."

"I'm sure it has, but this monster needs its treat. I could spend the rest of my life inside your body. You can suck me later…after you're rested, but right now, I need to be inside of you."

I gave a squeal as he lifted me and pressed me against the tile. I loved seeing him relax. All his hard edges disappeared. Not that I didn't like his hard edges, but I loved seeing this side of him too.

He was vulnerable and relaxed. I sensed those were two things he never allowed himself to be around others and treasured that he chose to share that side of himself with me. He needed more moments like this: tender moments, loving moments.

Times where he could simply be carefree.

Instead of a blowjob, I found myself with my legs once again wrapped around his hips as he fucked me against the wall of the shower.

He refused to let me dry myself, teasing me with the towel as he patted me dry. My last orgasm happened as I stood half dry in the bathroom with his head between my legs and his tongue doing wicked things.

"Why don't you get some rest?" he asked. "There are a few things I need to finish up."

There was no need to ask what he meant. His business arrangements needed to be finalized before that wretched man left the island. I snuggled under the covers and promptly fell asleep.

Sometime later, he woke me with a kiss and a smile which made the sea-green of his eyes glow. I wrapped my arms around his neck and pulled him close with the hopes this moment would never end.

"Stop," he said, "you need to get up."

"I don't want to get up." My stomach chose that moment to grumble, betraying me and reminding me I had skipped several meals.

"Your stomach says otherwise. Good thing, we have dinner."

"We?" I tugged at my lower lip. "Like you and me *we*, or others *we*?"

"Others."

"Do I have to?"

"That's up to you, but the invite is for tomorrow night. Carson has left the island, and I'm to meet him tomorrow to finalize everything."

"And watch the death matches." My stomach fluttered because I knew what would happen in that ring. It had to be stopped, but before Josh could bring down the operation, there would be boys who didn't survive. That thought gutted me. I wanted to save them all.

"This is something I can do without you. You can stay here."

"Won't it seem strange if you show up without your slave?"

"Probably, but it's not something you typically bring a date to."

"But I'm not a date. I'm your slave."

"You *were* my slave," he corrected.

"I know, but I bet he expects you to have me there. Not having me there shows weakness."

"How's that?"

"Because it would tell Carson you care about subjecting me to something like that. From what I understand, he gets off on watching others suffer. If you bring me, then he'll know you're exactly like him."

"Clara…" Josh pulled back, "I'm sorry I ever brought you into this world. You don't deserve it."

"The things you did…" I rushed to reassure him, "are things I've forgiven. I'll tell you that every day for the rest of my life until you believe me. I don't want to go. If I'm being totally honest, it scares me, but it's expected."

"I don't want you there. I can make an excuse."

"And raise his suspicions?"

"It's safest."

I didn't want to argue about this. The more we discussed it, the easier it would be for him to convince me I shouldn't go. Something told me that would be disastrous.

"Josh," I said his name to get his attention, "just answer one question. Don't think about it, just blurt out your answer."

"Okay?"

"Does Zane Carson expect your slave to be with you?"

"Absolutely."

"Then it's settled. I'm going."

He blew out his breath and pulled me into his arms.

"As long as you know the risks. I'll do everything to protect you, but we'll be flying without a safety net. The invitation is for me and me alone, and yes that invitation extends to my slave. But Clara…"

"Yes?"

"You may be forced to do things around others you're not comfortable doing. Don't you understand? Do you see why I don't want you there?"

"I do, and I understand. I was here when you killed Kate and Mitzy. Why wouldn't you bring me to this? Let's not talk about it anymore. We don't like it, but that's not why we're doing it."

He cupped my chin and stared at me with affection.

"I love how you want to save others."

"I love you, and I'm not doing anything. I'm just the eye candy. You're the hero for those boys."

"I don't know about that." He gave a low chuckle. "But you're definitely the finest eye candy I've ever seen. Now, let's get you dressed. It's time to meet the team."

"I think I'm more worried about meeting them than I am about tomorrow."

"Why's that?"

He'd told me everything about the rapes and how he tried framing his brother for murder, and what happened to Kate and Kevin's wife, Lily. He explained who Chambers was and how he was working for the FBI. Also, how Chambers was connected to Xavier who owned this expansive estate. Everything about Xavier's slave operation, and how he funneled slaves through it to freedom, had been explained.

What he didn't tell me worried me the most because none of

these people were his friends. They weren't even business associates. He'd been forced into his role by Kate, and I think Lily too, and worked under duress. I could only imagine the strained relationships surrounding him and how that must weigh on him.

He said nothing about his brother, Jake, which was the most revealing thing of all. I couldn't imagine the strain placed on their relationship.

Those people saw the man he'd been. They didn't know the amazing person he'd become. They didn't feel the comfort of his love, or the desperate need within him to be forgiven. He would never ask for it, but it was something he desperately needed. He would live with their hatred for the rest of his life, if only to spare them the nearly impossible act of forgiving him.

I might be the only person in the world who saw the true man behind the mask.

"Gimme a second to get dressed," I said, wishing it would just be us for dinner. If I could keep Josh to myself for the rest of my life, I'd be happy. I didn't want to share him with anyone, and I didn't want to subject him to the company of people who hated his guts.

"One second?" A mischievous glint flashed in his eye.

"Okay, five," I said with a laugh.

"If you're not ready in five seconds, you know where you're headed."

I glanced at his lap and his lusty gaze heated.

"If you put me over your lap, neither one of us is leaving this room until morning." My stomach gave a loud rumble as if to emphasize the point. "I'll hurry. How about that?"

"What am I supposed to do about this?" He pointed to his crotch and the very prominent swelling of his engorged cock.

"Are you superhuman? You spend more time with an erection than without."

"It's the filthy thoughts you put in my head. I'm constantly hard around you."

Since freeing me, we hadn't circled back around to anything

resembling our previous power dynamic. There had been no spankings, no orders, no demands that I obey.

Instead, we spent our time forging a new path, but sometime soon, we would circle back around to what brought us together. It was an eventuality; one I eagerly anticipated and cautiously avoided.

I wasn't ready for that yet, and I think he knew it.

"How about I beat off while I watch you dress?" He was also unabashed about stroking himself around me. I think it turned him on to catch me off guard, and he seemed to love making me blush. I did that now and the heat filling my cheeks had to have turned my face beet red.

I pointed to the closet. "I'm going to see what you brought from that chalet." The chalet he'd held me at happened to belong to Xavier as well. Kate might be the one running this operation, but Xavier had to be the one funding it. "I'll be out in a second."

"One second?" he teased.

"As many seconds as it takes, which means you don't have long to take care of that before dinner."

"I want to take care of it inside you."

"We don't have time for another shower."

"Why do you need a shower?"

"Because I don't want to meet these people with cum dripping down my legs."

"I don't mind that. I love the thought of my cum dripping down your legs while you meet them."

"I have no doubt you do, but the answer is no."

I hadn't meant to test him, but realized what happened the moment that word slipped out of my mouth.

Darkness flashed in Josh's expression and he turned away. He said nothing, which left me standing there feeling awkward and uncomfortable.

"I'm sorry. I didn't mean..."

He blew out a deep breath. "It's okay, Clara. We're going to stumble and trip over things which trigger us. You have every right to say no, and I respect it. I'll never force you to do anything again."

"I didn't mean it like that. I was just teasing…you know, playing?"

"I know. That word is a hard limit for me."

"A hard limit? I don't understand what that means."

"It's something we'll discuss later. But in consensual relationships each person has hard limits which are untouchable. We never discussed it before because you were…well, you were an unwilling participant."

"I'm not ready for that—"

"I know."

"No, you don't. You cut me off before I could finish. I'm not ready for that yet, but it's something I want to explore. It's a part of who you are, and I want to meet all your needs, and it may be a part of me too. I just don't know if it is."

"That means more to me than you know." He turned to me with a soft smile on his face. "One step at a time. Now, hurry up and get dressed. Take as long as you need."

"Okay."

I rushed to the closet and found something comfortable to wear. I assumed everyone had already seen me naked, which led me to choosing a more conservative dress. The white lace of the dress laid over a layer of thin white cotton. It had a high neck, mid-length sleeves, and came down to my knees. Conservative did not mean ugly or frumpy, however.

Josh had given me this dress. It was one I had earned for good behavior and it fit me like a glove, revealing more than it hid if I went by the expression on Josh's face when I exited the closet.

"You look…stunning."

"Thank you."

"I want to peel that dress off you right now, it looks that good."

"We're never leaving this room, are we?"

He reached down and adjusted the erection tenting his pants. "Unfortunately, they're waiting. But once this is all done, you and I are going away together where nobody can bother us and I'm going to spend all day and night fucking you."

"What a romantic," I teased.

"Well, not all day fucking you. There are a few things I want to try with the rope…" He let the rest of what he was going to say trail off as he opened the door. "After you, my sweet Clara."

Those three words, *my sweet Clara*, had me floating on Cloud Nine. I almost stopped to give him a peck on his cheek, but one look at the hunger in his eyes, and I decided to save that for later.

It was time to face a new threat—the family who hated him.

Chapter 8

Josh

It didn't take long to walk from my suite to the courtyard where dinner would be served. Word came through my phone that Carson and his goons had officially left the premises.

During our quick debrief while Clara slept, I received the unfortunate news that Mitzy had been unable to place the tracer on Carson's phone. This meant I would have to take care of that when I met with Carson tomorrow.

Snowden remained an elusive prize.

I said fuck it. I didn't care about Snowden. My goal was simple and personal. If I didn't rescue Wu's children, there would be no future with Clara. My head remained on a very real chopping block. Failure amounted to a death sentence. Success granted access to a new life.

If it hadn't been for that burden over my head, I would've stopped this whole thing the night I bought Clara and shut down the slave auction in Georgia.

"You seem tense?" Clara slipped her hand into mine and glanced up with concern.

"Sorry, I was just thinking about…stuff."

"Stuff?"

"Yeah…"

"I'm a good listener."

There was no doubt about that. Unloading my past, and admitting my sins to her, had been easier than I thought. Her quiet forgiveness of all the horrible things I'd done left me feeling lighter.

Unburdened might be a better word.

Renewed fit even better.

In her, I saw the reflection of the man I should have been all along: kind, caring, compassionate, and yes…even loving.

She made me feel whole.

Although, I hadn't shared everything. She still didn't know about my visit to Wu and the demand he made on me. No one knew that piece. I kept it close to my chest for obvious reasons. He provided the only escape from my previous life, a true out.

"I've burdened you enough."

"Okay." Her shoulders hunched inward.

I pulled up short, stopping us at the top of a landing overlooking one of Xavier's many courtyard gardens.

"I'll tell you everything." I drew her hands to my lips and kissed the backs of her knuckles. "There are still one or two things nobody knows. Things that aren't safe for you to know just yet, but I promise there'll be no secrets between us once this is all said and done."

"I believe you," she said, "and I didn't mean to press. I guess…I just thought this dinner might be hard for you. I wanted you to know that I believe in what you're doing."

"Thank you."

"Do they know that you told me?"

"They don't know, and they're going to throw a fit, but I don't give a damn. You'll never bow down to me again."

"Except for tomorrow…"

"Well, yeah, there's that." I hated that the idea of her kneeling before me made my cock twitch, but I couldn't help it.

"Is your brother going to be there?"

My breath hitched. I never specifically told her about the rift between Jake and I, but there hadn't really been a need. An idiot could have put those pieces together.

"Honestly, I don't know. Don't expect much out of him. He's not speaking to me."

"But he's involved…"

"Only because of Kate."

"If she's forgiven you, then he should too." She made it sound like the most obvious thing in the world, as if one magically followed the other. There was one problem with her logic. My brother hated me and Kate hadn't forgiven me.

I loved the fire in Clara's eyes and the way her hands clenched. I loved having someone on my side for the first time in my life.

"Kate hates my guts. It's kind of a family thing. Everyone hates me."

"I wish they could see you the way I do."

I did too, but that wasn't happening.

"I don't need that," I lied, "not when I can look in your eyes every day for the rest of my life."

I drew her into a hug, careful not to wake the raging beast inside my pants. I'd lost count of the number of times we'd fucked in the last twenty-four hours but suffice it to say there should be no reason to have blue balls. Except, I felt starved and needed another taste of her. I cut off our hug before my dick poked a hole through my pants.

"We should get going," I said.

"Tell me again who's going to be there. Kate, and your brother, Jake. I'm assuming the guy who owns this place. What was his name?"

"Xavier, and he has a slave named Raven." I suddenly realized one bit of info I failed to mention. "Um, you should know she's Carson's daughter."

"What?"

It took a moment to explain.

"That's a lot to take in. I guess Raven and I share common history. Well, except for the dad thing."

"How so?"

"We're both captives who fell in love. What do you think that says about us?"

"I think it shows how forgiving two amazing women can be. Maybe you two should talk?"

I'd love for her to sit with Raven and talk about her experience.

Clara said she had forgiven me, but I'd done some terrible shit to her. Having someone she could talk to about it, who understood, would be best.

That history would always be between us, and I didn't think Clara would ever be able to really tell me how she felt about some of the things I'd done.

Yes, I needed to get her and Raven together.

"I'd like that." I could see the gears churning in her head, and hoped some of those headed in the right direction. Clara would never give herself to me as a slave, but maybe she'd consider a close alternative.

"Okay, so Kate and Jake," she said, "Xavier and Raven, they're Master/slave pairs?"

"Yes. Mitzy will be there too. She's Kate's assistant and the first girl you watched me kill. Of course, you know Chambers."

"It makes sense he's FBI. It fits him."

"Well, he's also submissive to Xavier, or a slave. Honestly, I don't know how that dynamic works. He, Abrams—he's the one who posed as Chambers business associate—as well as the two guards, Bay and Chad, are all bonded to Xavier."

"You're right. I don't understand that. Is that it?"

"I don't know if Forest's medical team is still on the island or not."

"Who?"

"Forest. He's a computer geek."

"That's a lot of people."

"I suppose, but like I said, I think the medical team left."

"I'd like to be a fly on that wall," she said.

"Which wall?"

"The one where the medical team got together to figure out how to fake a person's death and revive them. That's pretty intense."

"Maybe you'll have a chance to meet them someday." If I had it my way, Clara would never be anywhere near these people again.

Forest had a bug up his butt about Snowden, and he was clearly gearing up for a major operation to take the man down. I wanted nothing to do with that. My participation in this shit show ended with the safe return of Wu's children. After that, I planned on disappearing. My family didn't need me around as a constant reminder of what I'd done.

"You ready?" I kissed the top of her head. There was only one staircase and two hallways to traverse before we arrived at the central courtyard and a very odd dinner.

"Absolutely."

With her hand in mine, I led her the rest of the way. The last people to arrive, everyone stopped what they were doing and looked up. Not one damn smile, not that I expected any.

They were all there, sitting around a massive table, breaking bread and shooting the shit. At least, they had been. I took one step into the space and the entire vibe shifted.

My hand tightened on Clara's hand.

"Tough crowd." She reached over with her free hand and gripped my bicep.

Her comment brought a smile to my face. Only Clara could break that tension.

"Good evening everyone." I pulled her into the room. "May I introduce Clara."

Xavier shifted in his seat at the head of the table. Raven sat in a chair immediately to his left. Jake sat to his right with Kate beside him. I expected Xavier to say something. As host, it was his right. Mitzy sat next to Kate and Chambers was across the table from her. There was only one place setting left at the foot of the table

My brother fixed me with a glare. "Your slave is not required at this meeting." He couldn't have given a stiffer brush off, but I was prepared. "Send her away."

"Clara is not my slave." From the expressions on everyone's faces, that got their attention. "Furthermore, she knows."

"Shit, Josh!" Kate slapped her napkin down on the table. "This is not what we discussed."

"I don't give a shit what we discussed. Clara is free to do as she pleases."

Xavier coughed into his fist. "Miss Clara, one day I hope you forgive what happened to you. In the meantime, I'll arrange for your immediate departure. We have a process—"

"Oh, I know about your process." She hugged my arm. "Josh told me all about it. Thank you, but it won't be necessary."

"Excuse me?" Xavier said. "You're free to go. We'll help you start over."

"I'm staying with Josh." She glanced up at me with absolute adoration and gave a loving wink. I couldn't help but grin. My girl was having fun with this.

"She's deranged," Kate said. "Hun, you're suffering from Stockholm syndrome."

Raven glanced at Xavier and gave a soft smile. He reached out and took her hand in his. Yeah, they understood. But Xavier said nothing.

Meanwhile, Clara's voice rose, but her tone held steady. My girl was on a roll and I couldn't love her more than I did at that moment.

"I'm not suffering anything, and I'm most certainly not deranged. Josh explained everything. I'm staying with him."

I wanted to give her the biggest high five and follow it with the sloppiest kiss in the world. She was the first person who ever stood up for me, or stood by me.

"Well, your role in this is finished," Kate said. "And once you figure out what kind of monster he is, you'll regret your decision to stay."

"I don't think you understand. I've forgiven him. I love him, and I'm going with him tomorrow. It's what Carson expects."

"Absolutely not." Kate pushed away from the table and shot to her feet. "That's not happening. The only reason we used you was because we needed the honest reaction of a woman Josh brutalized. Carson will know the difference. You can't go."

"Well, at least we got that out of the way," Clara said. "And as for being brutalized, you're the one who set me up. Not Josh. He wanted nothing to do with any of this. He would have been happy leaving that prison and disappearing to lead a quiet life, but you coerced him into doing it. You stole his money…"

"We did no such thing."

"Bullshit. You took his money, bullied him into helping you, and left him no choice. If anyone is a monster, it's you."

"Me?"

"Yes!" Clara's shoulders rolled back, and she puffed out her chest. "You knew I'd been abducted, along with the others. You could have rescued us. Instead, you let the auction proceed. I was nearly raped that night."

She clutched my arm. "But he saved me." Clara pointed to my brother. "Your brother saved me from being raped the night of that auction. He did that. You and your little crew here would have let that happen by your negligence to rescue me when you had the chance. And not once did Josh force himself on me. I ask this…who in this room are the real monsters? Because from my standpoint, it's all of you."

"Clara…" I tried to hush her, but the look she gave me told me everything I needed to know. Clara was on a roll and she had something to say.

"Although Josh had ample opportunity to rape me, he didn't. And that's not the end of it. *You* forced Josh into a position where he had to make me a slave. It wasn't something he chose and not something he agreed with. He knew what that would do to me, but you left him with no choice. You're the monsters, not him."

She let go of my hand and crossed her arms over her chest, defiant, proud, and ready to take on the world. "And tomorrow, Josh and I are going to end this…together."

"This is insane." Kate turned to Xavier. "Aren't you going to say something?"

Xavier took a moment to study Clara. His gaze dipped to her hand and the way she clutched my arm. He had to have noticed how she stood beside me, with no gap between our bodies…by her choice. Not because I threatened her. Not because I forced her. But because she chose me.

My heart tripped a little.

Clara chose me.

Despite everything, she found it within herself to look beyond the mistakes of my past and see me. Forgave me, the man who deserved nothing.

"I think this is something we should discuss." Xavier tapped his finger on the tablecloth.

"There's no discussion," Clara said, "I'm going."

"I didn't say you wouldn't, only that we needed to discuss it. Kate has valid concerns. Carson knows the difference between a true slave and an act. That puts your life in danger."

"It won't be an act." She jutted out her chin.

"I didn't say it would be, Miss Clara." He gestured to the table and the empty place setting at the far end. "Chambers, please set another place."

"Yes, Sir." Chambers jumped up, obeying instantly.

"Please, let's enjoy a civil dinner, then we'll discuss what happens next." Xavier gestured to the empty chair.

"You're not the boss of me," she said.

"Clara…" I leaned down to whisper in her ear. "This isn't the time to force the issue."

"But…"

"We're Xavier's guests." I threaded my fingers with hers and gave a tug toward our seats. "Let's not disrespect him in his house."

Xavier heard me and gave a slight nod of respect. He was the one Clara had to convince, not the others, and I had a pretty good idea he would be eating out of the palm of her hand before the evening was done. He understood what Clara had been through, and maybe he understood a little about me.

Either way, there was no doubt in my mind whether Clara would join me.

Chapter 9

Clara

I'd entered a fresh, new level of hell. Unlike Xavier's tropical island, none of this was pretend. Early in the morning, Josh and I boarded Xavier's jet and flew somewhere in Bangladesh.

Covered head to toe, I respected local custom while transferred into a dark SUV and traveled bumpy roads until we arrived in a compound surrounded by ten-foot concrete walls; a compound with an ornate estate and a series of warehouses.

We sat in one now; the others housed the slaves.

Carson treated us like royalty. Or rather, he treated Josh like royalty.

I was nothing.

Not that Carson didn't spend an inordinate amount of time staring at me. The heat of his gaze lifted the fine hairs on my nape and made my skin crawl. Josh kept a hand on me at all times, and I played the role of meek slave perfectly.

All those weeks of training made it easy to slip back into that mode. I kept my head bowed, refused to make direct eye contact, and replied *Yes, Sir* to every command and every response.

We sat on a raised platform. I'd call it a dais but it wasn't that ornate. A boxing ring sat in the middle of the space with bleachers all around, and there was a crowd of over fifty men who shouted at the boys in the ring. Women circulated amongst the crowd, delivering beverages and smokes to greedy bastards.

Meanwhile, I shuddered at the ghastly sight of children forced to kill.

Josh didn't want me here. I should have listened. I should have obeyed. I never should have forced him to bring me with him.

This is something I can do without you.

He had tried to protect me from this vileness, but I foolishly thought we should continue pretending. How real, or fake, that might become in the future wasn't something I was ready to face, but I could pretend. And from the way Carson kept looking at me, I made the right choice.

Those were problems for another day.

For now?

A hushed shock permeated the crowd. The savage fury of the previous participants still rang in the air. The fight lasted far too long, and yet at the same time had been incredibly short. The victor swayed on his feet, moving back and forth, panting and confused. Almost as if he didn't believe he'd taken a life. Or maybe, he was surprised he still lived?

His first life, if I could believe what Carson said. This boy was fresh off the streets, pushed into a battle with only one survivor. The other boy's body lay bloody and still. His dead eyes stared at the ceiling.

Panic overwhelmed me. My decision to be here turned into a fit of doubt, but there was no going back. I trusted Josh. I believed in him and what he was trying to accomplish. He warned me.

We can't save them all.

What I wouldn't give to reverse time, save that poor boy's life, and save the victor from the knowledge he was now a killer.

The boy teetered back and forth, his gaze vacant and his face expressionless. When he realized what he'd been forced to do, what would it do to him? He may be the victor, but he was also a victim.

My heart went out to him.

"Impressive," Carson said, "I didn't think he would win."

"People can surprise you," Josh said. "Did you bet against him?"

Carson shook his head. "That kid is fresh. Plucked off the streets not two days ago. I figured he would be easy meat. He took down one of our up and coming fighters. I guess that's a surprise, even if it cost me ten thousand."

Ten thousand?

I tried not to react, but he'd bet ten-thousand dollars on that kid's life? Did the man have no humanity left within him? Strike that question. I knew the answer.

"How do you find them?" Josh asked.

"The same as you. Runaways with no family to miss them."

That hurt more than it should. There would be no one to mourn these children. The boy wobbling in the middle of the ring came from nothing, and he'd been used as nothing other than sacrificial meat for men willing to pay to watch him die.

Or live.

Today he lived.

"This is a fresh batch." Carson said. "We've recently expanded operations."

"They look Taiwanese." Josh glanced down at the girl huddled by Carson's feet.

Carson wrapped his fingers in the girl's hair and gave a tug. Tears pooled in her defeated eyes, and she didn't resist as he manhandled her into his lap and stole a kiss. A slip of a girl, she couldn't be legal. Although, why I thought age meant anything to these men, escaped me.

The poor thing looked to be in her early teens.

I clutched Josh's hand and trembled at his feet. As his slave, I dutifully knelt beside him.

The boy in the ring swayed while the crowd around him buzzed as they settled their debts or collected their payouts.

Two men entered the ring. One dragged the dead boy out, while the other slapped handcuffs on the boy and pushed him out of the ring. The boy stumbled and was bodily lifted back to his feet. He shuffled between a set of raised bleachers, while those in the stands craned their necks, whispering about the victor. The boy disappeared behind a set of metal doors and I let out my breath.

Josh placed his hand over mine, saying nothing, but providing all the strength I needed to get through this.

Something ate at him. He kept looking to the girl in Carson's lap. The corners of his lips twitched.

Disembodied logic ran through my mind. This charade was necessary because Carson didn't work alone. Josh hoped to meet Carson's business partner.

I shut my eyes, thankful the worst part of this night was over.

But then the doors reopened.

Two more boys were pushed toward the ring. One of them looked eerily similar to the girl sitting in Carson's lap.

The boy's attention shifted to the girl. The scowl on his face deepened as fury bunched his muscles. Carson yanked on the girl's hair. Her scream made the boy stumble and his fists curl.

"That one…" Carson pointed to the boy, "is this one's brother. What do you think about that, slave? You ready to watch your brother die? Or, do you think he'll win again?"

Again?

That boy had already survived the ring?

My soul wept for the horrors inflicted on these children. And clearly, the evening was far from over.

"A brother and sister," Josh said, "that's unusual."

"It's fucking brilliant."

"I only meant it's unusual for siblings to runaway together."

"Oh, these didn't run away."

"Is that so?"

Carson gave a snort. "These two are paying for their father's arrogance. A man who thinks he's untouchable." He yanked on the girl's hair again and tears trickled down her cheeks. "What do you think about that, slave? Your father knows I have you. All he had to do was take one step back. Instead, he did nothing. That's what you mean to your father. You mean nothing."

The girl whimpered. From the extensive bruising on her body, and the various stages of healing, I understood the torture she'd endured.

Josh looked pissed. "That seems reckless. Kidnapping brings the wrong kind of attention."

"Oh, I don't know about that. Sometimes it brings interesting results."

The boys reached the ring and were prodded to enter. I was certain they understood what happened next. One of them would be bludgeoned to death. The other would be stripped of his humanity. I could already see it in the brother's eyes.

He was resigned.

"This is not his first time in the ring then?" Josh asked the obvious.

"This is his third fight. He barely survived the second. I think this will be interesting. Are you willing to place a bet?"

"Maybe later."

"But I thought this is what you craved? You look like you're going to be sick. Maybe this isn't for you?"

Josh's body tensed. "You've seen what I'm capable of…"

"Yes, I have at that." Carson pushed the girl out of his lap and settled back into his chair. "I think this will be interesting."

The size of the crowd surprised me, not that the room was overflowing with men, but there had to be over forty people in the stands. How much did each of them pay to secure a seat? Let alone the betting pool.

My heart vibrated in my chest, rattled up my neck, and pulsed in my skull as the officiator of the fight read out the boys' statistics. They had both survived two previous matches. It was cruel to pit them against each other, although why I thought this was worse than the previous fight didn't make sense.

I think my mind struggled to make sense of an insane situation.

The idle chatter in the stands rose in waves, reaching a crescendo as the officiator came to the end of the stats for the boys. There wasn't a single woman with the men, although there were several working the stands, selling refreshments. They had to be slaves as well.

A sense of anticipation built to a crescendo as if this fight held more significance than the previous one. Why that may be, remained a mystery. There would be the same blood spilled.

The crowd began chanting. Their excitement grew as my guts twisted with the depravity of it all. Shame filled me that humans could be this evil and take pleasure in the destruction of others.

The air vibrated against my skin with the thrum of anticipation for blood. Perspiration beaded on my brow, and I couldn't help but shiver.

The boys in the ring tightened their fists. Any moment now, they would begin. I looked at them and saw the moment a switch flipped inside of them as they mentally prepared to live or die.

Evenly matched, my gut told me this wouldn't be quick. The moment the bell clanked, the boys launched at each other, flinging fists and feet in a desperate attempt to score early hits.

The noise of the crowd rushed through me, slamming into me with what felt like a physical force. I clutched my stomach.

"Are you going to be okay?" Josh leaned down and whispered in my ear.

I gave a slight nod, then remembered my assumed role. "Yes, Sir, just a little queasy." My heart thundered, banging away inside my chest like a kettle drum.

With the first punches out of the way, the boys squared off against each other. The girl's brother danced around his opponent, keeping his footfalls light as he dodged. But he kept looking over at his sister.

That distraction cost him.

The other boy jabbed, landing a punch in the gut. He followed it up with a cut to the solar plexus, then a slam to the temple. The girl's brother stumbled, gave a shake of his head, then fell to the mat. His opponent took the opportunity to attack, raining down fists and kicking him in the ribs.

The brother curled into a fetal ball, guarding his vulnerable areas. But the other kid kicked him in the stomach. The powerful thrust lifted the boy off the floor and tossed him to the side. He gasped for breath as his sister cried out.

Carson tossed the girl to the side and barked out an order to one of the guards flanking us. His personal guards, the two men intimidated me with their size.

"Get her out of here." He kicked the girl as she scrabbled away.

One of the men hoisted her by the waist and tossed her over his shoulder. She cried out and lifted her arms toward her brother, saying something I didn't understand.

The guard left the room with the girl, then returned moments later without her. Instead of taking up his position from before, he moved around to stand beside me. His fierce expression focused forward as I shifted closer to Josh.

Punches rained down on her brother, then the other boy turned into something feral. He grabbed the brother from behind and wrapped an arm around his neck. He used his strength to hold the arm bar while the boy's face turned red.

I wanted to scream, *He's killing him!* But that was the point of this dreadful event. The kid squeezed and the brother's face turned purple as he flailed and scratched. In a few more seconds, he would pass out.

No.

He wouldn't pass out.

He would be strangled by a boy given no other choice than to kill.

Tension built in Josh's body. I felt it in the tightening of his leg muscles. In the stillness of his breath, and in the deadly quiet girding his frame.

"I wonder what his father would think, knowing you watched his son die."

"Excuse me?" Josh put a hand on my shoulder and pushed me to the side.

The man beside me took a step closer.

"Please," Carson said with a sneer. "Do you think I'm an idiot?"

"I think you're a lot of things."

"Really? But tell me, are you willing to let Wu's son die?"

"You're a monster."

"Says the man who killed two women."

The muscles in Josh's jaw bunched. "Kate deserved to die."

"I'll give you that."

The brother weakened in the stranglehold.

"Let the boy go."

"So, you admit you're working for Wu?"

"Wu wants me dead."

"That's not what I hear."

"I don't care what you think you heard. I've had enough of this."

Carson waved to the crowd. "They're here to watch a fight to the death. I'm not going to disappoint them."

Josh pulled out a gun and pointed it at Carson's chest.

"Let him go."

The guard beside me leapt forward. He scooped me off my feet and put a knife to my throat.

My entire body stilled as the hard edge of the blade cut into my skin. A warm trickle of blood ran along my collar bone and dripped between my breasts. A surface cut, it was meant to make a point.

"Now, isn't this interesting." Carson gave a low chuckle. "Me or the girl? I wonder who you'll pick?"

"She's just a slave."

"Let's have some fun. You get to decide who lives and dies tonight."

"Maybe you're not understanding me." Josh's finger went for the trigger. "You're not making it out of here alive. That's a promise."

Carson gave a slow shake of his head. "You're not going to kill me."

"You don't know me very well. I keep my promises."

Carson jerked his chin in the direction of the brother fighting for his life. "How about this? You take that boy's place in the ring. I let him and the girl live."

"I'm not fighting a child, asshole."

"Oh, I don't intend for you to fight the boy. Two lives require a bit more sport than that." He gestured to his guards. "You'll fight them…to the death."

Josh looked at me and, despite the knife at my throat, I gave a hard swallow. I didn't see the monster inside of him. I saw a raging beast.

He didn't hesitate and lowered the gun.

"Deal."

Carson looked surprised, but then murder gleamed in his eyes. He raised his hands and gave a loud clap. "Stop the fight!"

The other guard disarmed Josh, then pushed him toward the ring. The one holding me pushed me toward Carson. He shoved me into Carson's waiting arms then handed over the knife.

Shocked by the turn in events, my body moved on autopilot.

Please don't die.

I didn't know if Josh heard me, but he glanced back as he willingly climbed into the ring. He had no words for me, but then he couldn't let Carson know the truth between us.

"You're a dead man, Zane Carson. Dead." Josh rolled up his sleeves.

Carson twisted my arm behind my back. With the knife pressed against my neck, he whispered vileness into my ear. "I'm going to do unspeakable things to you, my darling slave."

The boys were separated and the brother coughed in a breath. Strength returned to him slowly, and he gave Josh a wary look as the two of them exchanged positions.

Josh rolled his shoulders back and flexed his muscles. His fingers curled and a snarl lifted his upper lip. The two guards strutted toward the ring, followed by cheering from the crowd and a flurry of new betting.

Careful not to let Carson see, I mouthed *I love you* to Josh.

His lips moved. *I love you more.*

Chapter 10

Josh

My teeth slammed together with enough force to rattle my brain. Pain exploded behind my eyes and fire erupted over my jaw. My face caught the worst of the assault. The skin over my cheek split and blood dripped down to my chin.

A coppery tang coated my tongue, blood from where I'd bit through the inside of my cheek. A cut across my forehead bled and the blood mingled with my sweat.

Rivulets of agony poured down my face.

Carson was going to die for this, but first I needed to get through his guards and the crowd of vile and filth, the worst humanity had to offer who cheered for blood, sweat, and death.

A chop to my solar plexus made the act of breathing impossible, but these men had no idea what I was. They hadn't survived what I had endured, or trained to beat it.

I spit blood onto the mat and blinked to clear my vision. Not that I needed to see. All my senses were on high alert. I tracked my opponents by sound more than sight. I had to. With the two of them, they found all my blind spots, working them to their advantage.

They didn't know how foolish that was, or what it would cost them. I would take their pummeling, saving my strength for when it mattered most. This was just a warmup, the three of us dancing around the ring like tweens at our first awkward dance.

A slight creak sounded behind me. The mat shifted as the bastard behind launched a roundhouse kick to the back of my knee. A blind grab put his leg in my hands. Using his momentum, I yanked him forward and off his feet. His foot, ankle and shin twisted. His knee and the rest of his body did not.

A loud *pop* preceded his agonized scream as the ligaments of his knee shredded. He went down and stayed there.

Now, there was only one man standing between me and Zane Carson.

One man and one woman.

Carson held my sweet Clara in front of him. He had an arm wrapped around her, trapping her arms to her side, and pressed a knife to her goddamn throat. I was going to kill the bastard.

She had looked at me with fear twisting her delicate features as Carson ordered my death in the most diabolical way possible. A fight to the death in the same ring as Wu's son, a boy turned into a man too soon, forced to kill or die. They had carried him away, back to the pens where he would recover until his next match. Or so I assumed.

But if I survived this shit, there would be no next match, and we would all be walking out of here.

Clara should not have been here. My weakness placed her in danger. And now, if I didn't survive, she would enter a living hell as one of Carson's many pleasure slaves. There was no illusion on my part as to what he would force her to endure.

You're a dead man walking!

My distraction cost me. The other guard advanced, fists flying, as I blinked to clear my vision. He got in some good hits, pounding on me like he was tenderizing raw meat. The flurry of his fists kept me battling for breath and I staggered under a particularly devastating series of blows. Fortunately, he shuffled back to catch his breath and I sucked in air.

The noise from the crowd returned, hungry cries for blood and death filled the air from outside the makeshift ring. There weren't that many, but more than I could take on alone. They cheered for my death from all angles, but they would be disappointed.

I was a tough bastard to kill.

The wounded man on the mat clutched at his knee while Carson screamed at him to get up. The throbbing in my ears siphoned out the crowd's chants and allowed me to focus on the solid beating of my heart.

Whomp—whomp—whomp.

My heart forced blood through my body, delivering oxygen to my starved muscles. My entire body pulsed to the rhythm, centering my mind and keeping me on my toes.

But it wasn't enough.

My head snapped back with another upper cut to my jaw.

Blood gushed from my nose and poured down my throat, choking me, and coating my senses with the coppery flavor of defeat. The man on the mat swung out, trying to trip me, but I danced over his arm and kicked him in the head.

His head bounced against the mat and then his entire body stilled. I didn't know if I'd killed him or knocked him out cold, but now was not the time to figure that shit out.

With a shake of my head, I forced myself to get back in the game.

Focus!

Carson had Clara.

I had to get to her. I would die trying.

Falling back on instinct, knees bent, weight centered on the balls of my feet, I found my balance and waited for a surge of adrenaline to spike through me. My opponent got in a few knocks to my ribs. I tensed and absorbed the blows as he launched forward with a fist aimed at my solar plexus.

Instead of letting his fist connect with my chest, my arm snapped forward and my fingers wrapped around his wrist. With a yank, I pulled him toward me, spinning at the last minute to avoid full frontal contact.

Once again, I used momentum to my advantage.

The man stumbled in a drunken dance and went down, face first. He flopped over and tried to stand.

Blood drenched my knuckles, proof I'd scored a few direct hits, but it wasn't enough.

I dropped to my knees, straddling my opponent, and pulverized his body. I chopped at his muscular frame, hammering my fists into his stomach as I aimed to split his spleen.

Fuck. I needed to end this.

I needed a killing blow.

Each swing of my fists seemed to come slower than the last. My body was tiring, but I wasn't ready to give up.

With my heart hammering, I blinked through a mess of blood and sweat, I remembered a similar situation, the night I saved Clara.

I located my target and slammed the base of my palm against his windpipe. His head snapped back as the cartilage gave way with a sickening *crunch*.

A shot rang in my ears and pain exploded in my arm.

The sharp burst of sensation spiked through my brain and bowled me over with a howl of pain and frustration. I'd been shot from the asshole with the busted-up knee. Where the fuck did he get a gun?

The noise from the crowd shifted. Instead of shouts, low grumbles filled the room. These men paid for death matches played out with nothing but bare fists. The grumbling turned ominous as their displeasure raced through the room.

Perhaps I should be thankful they didn't approve of bringing a gun into this fight. I could use that to my advantage.

I spit new blood onto the mat.

Never taking my eyes off my opponent, I clutched at my wounded arm and waited for him to breathe. His vacant eyes stared at the ceiling and I removed him from the list of imminent threats. Then I turned to the wounded man.

He shifted to his butt. His ruined knee twisted at an unnatural angle. And his hands shook as he held the gun.

"Do it!" Carson shouted from the stands. "Kill him!"

The grumbling from the crowd grew as men exchanged angry shouts. Everyone in this wretched space had something to lose. If they were smart, they were debating their next move. As long as they got their show, no one gave a fuck who died.

Win or lose, I would live or die. I rushed my opponent as he pulled the trigger. A shot rang out and Clara screamed. Pain bit at my injured arm, but I was beyond caring.

A hasty lunge and I missed. Bad timing on my part as he rolled out of the way. But my fist found his ribs. One of them gave beneath my knuckles and knocked the wind from his lungs.

I kicked the gun out of his hands and rained a storm of fury down on him, pelting him with my fists despite the pain in my injured arm.

Crack—crack—crack!

His chest caved in as I hammered into him, cutting off his oxygen and starving his brain with the hopes he'd black out. I didn't *want* to kill him, but I would.

However, my strength was fading fast. Battered and breathless with an injury to my arm, I wasn't going to last much longer. My enemy weakened, but would it be fast enough?

He blocked me. I wore him down, measuring out the remnants of my strength as I desperately wished for him to simply give up. Finally, his arms dropped beneath my strikes, opening him to attack.

Desperation and fear mingled in the air, bringing a sour taste to my mouth. This might be it. But I wouldn't stop, not until Carson was dead.

I drew back and wheezed in a breath, filling my lungs with hatred for Carson. My ravaged knuckles beat against the bloody mess of my opponent's face until his body went still.

I turned to Carson and watched with satisfaction as his expression changed. His complexion paled and fear took root in his eyes.

I lunged for the gun as he pressed the switchblade to Clara's neck.

The moment caught me unaware and an odd sensation rushed through me as everything precious in my life hung in the moment.

Was this what Jake felt when our father held the knife to Kate's throat? This fear and helplessness? The rage?

Only, I wasn't helpless, and rage fed my beast.

When a man has everything to lose, he'll do anything to win.

No longer hindered by Carson's sick and twisted game, I took one breath to steady my hand.

I lifted the gun.

"Shoot and the girl dies." Carson's voice shook nearly as hard as his hand holding the knife.

If there was noise from the crowd, I couldn't hear it. My entire existence narrowed down to three things.

Me.

The barrel of the gun.

And the path the bullet would take.

Chapter 11

Josh

Something dark and inhuman shifted inside of me. The beast roared, demanding Carson's blood. My lips spread into a smile and I pulled the trigger.

One moment Carson stood with a knife held to Clara's throat. The next, his body crumpled to the ground. I may have imagined the widening of his eyes as the shock of the bullet penetrated his skull. It mattered that he knew I had won, but I would never be certain if that had been real or something imagined.

As for Clara?

Carson's knife sliced across her neck and shoulder, but she was safe.

She was alive.

I turned on the crowd.

"Who the fuck is next?"

Not one man answered. A mob of cowards, they panicked and ran. I staggered to my feet, waving the gun as I searched for threats.

In my peripheral vision, Clara grabbed at her neck. A rivulet of blood dripped from the cut at her throat, and the whites showed around her eyes, but she appeared steady on her feet.

The same could not be said of Carson.

Eyes staring blankly at the ceiling, the motherfucker was dead.

I held the gun and searched for guards. Instead of jumping in and taking me down, or better yet putting a bullet in my head, they ran out of the room with the cowardly mob.

So much for loyalty.

I needed to act fast.

Jumping over the ropes, I rushed to Clara's side. Removing my shirt, I thrust it at her.

"Put this on." My shirt would hang halfway to her knees and cover her as best I could. "Are you okay?"

I glanced at her neck and took a look at the cut. Clean and shallow, it didn't look as bad close up as it had from the ring. It would need stitches, but not immediate medical care.

"It's barely a scratch."

My girl was so damn strong.

Bending down, I rifled through Carson's pockets looking for his phone. Putting a tracer on it seemed a moot point with him dead, but maybe Mitzy or Forest could salvage something from it in their search for Snowden. Meanwhile, I had other more important things to take care of…like getting the hell out of this place.

I checked the clip, counted the remaining bullets, and prayed I wouldn't need any of them. Not knowing what waited for us outside, I prepared for the worst.

We didn't have time to waste, but I went to the two dead guards on the mat to see if they had any other weapons. I pulled a revolver off one and found a second clip on the other.

"Let's go."

Clara glanced at me. "Where are we going?"

Fear simmered in her eyes and she appeared reluctant to leave the safety of the building.

"It's not safe here. We need to move."

I didn't know what we'd find outside, and I didn't have a way to contact Xavier. My cellphone had been confiscated—*standard procedure, you understand*—before they allowed us inside.

Keeping Clara close, hugged to my side and a little behind me, I pushed on the door leading outside. The bin where all the cell phones had been standing was knocked over on the ground. Dozens of abandoned cell phones littered the ground.

"See if you can find my phone." I needed to get word out to Xavier that this whole thing had gone to shit.

Standing guard over Clara while she searched, I peered through the darkness toward the other buildings. There were too many to search, but Wu's children had to be inside one, or two, of them. It would make sense to keep the boys and girls separate.

Fuck my life.

I couldn't return with only one of them.

Think!

"Found it!" Clara lifted my phone triumphantly.

"Shh…" We didn't need to attract attention.

"Sorry." She lowered her voice. "What now?" She searched the small parking lot and I followed her gaze. Our ride had disappeared in the chaos. Then I saw what I needed.

A worn path in the dirt.

I took my phone from her and hit the flashlight to examine the ground. Deep boot imprints intermingled with smaller footprints. They led toward the back buildings.

We were sitting ducks outside. Anyone could take us out, but I betted on everyone running. Whoever Carson hired for security needed to be fired, but from the absence of any guards, he clearly only had security for himself. I had taken those men out.

I headed toward the outbuildings.

"What are you doing?" Clara kept her voice down and hunched beside me.

"I need to get Malee and Maceo."

"Who?"

"Carson's slave and that boy."

She gave me a look.

"I'll explain later." Gripping her hand, I picked up our pace. She kept right by my side.

We stopped at the first building. Locked.

Shit.

I gave three sharp kicks and busted through the lock. The door opened on a dark interior with long rows of fenced cages. About a dozen girls backed away and huddled in the corners.

"Oh my God!" Clara reached for one of the cages and tugged at a lock.

I pulled her hand back. "We need to find Malee."

"But…"

I thrust out my phone. "Call Xavier. He'll take care of this, but we don't have time to free them."

She took the cell phone with a shaky hand, but didn't hesitate to punch in the numbers to the burner phone Xavier set up for *contingencies*. While she told him what happened, I searched the cages.

But I didn't find Malee.

Clara trailed behind me snippets of her conversation with Xavier reached my ears. I waved for her to follow me and ignored the desperate faces looking out from the cages.

You can't save them all.

But damn if I didn't want to try.

Xavier and his team would have to handle it. Wu's children's lives, and by extension, mine, were on the line.

"Let's keep going."

Clara kept the phone next to her ear as her head swiveled back and forth, looking for Wu's daughter. There was something oddly fulfilling about having Clara work beside me, rather than serving beneath me. We were a team, and that did strange things to my head and my heart.

I had so much more to lose than a few days ago.

We exited the first building and moved on to the next.

This one held cages of boys.

Unlike the girls, they came to the front of their cells, fingers clawing through the wire chain links. Their defiant eyes stared with lethal menace and hatred. While we didn't have time for it, I knew there was only one way to truly save those other girls.

"Clara!"

"Yes?"

"Look along the wall for the keys."

She didn't hesitate.

I spoke to the boys in English and then in Thai. *"We're here to free you."*

Their angry expressions hardened, not with fear but mistrust. I didn't have time for that shit. As I raced down the cages, I called out Maceo's name, and told the boys they needed to save the girls in the other building.

"How far out?" I turned to Clara.

"Ten minutes."

I had ten minutes to locate Malee and Maceo before Xavier's extraction team arrived. A contingency they prepared to get Clara and I out if things went south. I planned to add two more people to that count.

As for the others? I didn't know what to do about them.

One of the boys spoke to me in English.

"You're looking for Maceo?" He had to be seventeen or eighteen because his body had begun to take on the bulky muscles of a man. But looking into his eyes, I didn't see a boy. A saw someone forced to grow up far too soon.

"Yes!"

"Did he survive his fight?"

"Yes." At the crestfallen look on his face, I rushed to reassure him. "They both did. I stopped it."

"You?"

"Where is Maceo?"

"They take us to the infirmary after a fight." What did these boys do while waiting for their next battle? Did they talk to one another? Or did they retreat into themselves, refusing to forge friendships in such a desolate place?

Deep-seated anger stirred within me at the hell these boys had been subjected to, and I itched to do something to help them.

"Found it!" Clara called out.

"Bring it here." I looked to the boy. "Free as many as you can, and don't you dare forget the girls in the next building. Protect them."

When Clara arrived, I took the key and waited for the boy to acknowledge what I said. When he gave a cautious nod, I unlocked his cell and placed the key in his hand.

"What's your name?"

"Marcus."

"Well, Marcus, they're your responsibility. There's a team coming to take us out, but you're going to have to help everyone until they get here. You're on your own. Don't forget the girls."

"I won't." His chest puffed out with purpose.

I hesitated, knowing he couldn't do it on his own, but I had my own agenda. Knowing nothing about him, but having a good idea how he wound up here, I did the next best thing.

"Is there anyone I can get a message to?"

"There's no one who cares." He shook his head then rolled his shoulders back. "Infirmary is the second building to the left. Out that door."

Clara threaded her fingers with mine and pressed against me.

"Josh, we need to go."

Without another word, we headed out the back door. The second building to the left was much smaller than the others. It didn't have a lock. I lifted my weapon while Clara opened the door.

An examination table filled the center of the room and a row of cabinets lined the back wall. To the left, a large wire-link cage held a boy.

"Maceo!" I couldn't believe it. I found him. "Where's your sister?" Wu's children attended exclusive private schools and had learned English from an early age.

"What do you want with my sister?"

There wasn't time to search for a key, and I had a feeling whoever held it had fled with the others. I turned my gun on the lock, and Maceo brought his hands up, guarding his body. Ignoring him, I pulled the trigger and shot off the lock.

With a yank, I jerked it free and opened the cage.

"We have to hurry. Do you or do you not know where your sister is?"

"Who are you?"

"Your father sent me. Now, where is Malee?"

"That sick bastard kept her at the main house."

"Show me." I glanced down at his bare feet and hoped that wouldn't slow us down.

With Clara tucked to my side, the three of us worked our way to the main house. Clara kept in contact with Xavier by phone while Maceo and I slipped between the shadows.

"I've seen them take her in there, but I don't know where they keep her." He pointed to a side door.

Shit, I didn't want to have to search an entire house.

"Two minutes out," Clara announced.

Our combined gaze turned to the night sky, seeking the lights of the helicopter which would take us from this place.

"Let's go."

"They want us to meet them at the parking lot." Clara glanced toward the building where the fights had been held and pulled away from me.

There was no way she would leave my side. I still didn't know if there were other guards roaming around.

I turned to Maceo. "Do you know how to use a gun?"

The teen shook his head.

"I do." Clara spoke up.

"You?"

"Yes." She pointed to the revolver I had shoved beneath the waistband of my pants next to my lower back. "I'm a really good shot. Give me that."

"Are you sure?"

She spoke into the phone. "I'm giving you to a…" she hesitated, "…a friend."

Maceo took the phone. "Hello?"

Clara waited for me to hand over the revolver, which I was grateful for. If she'd reached for it, she could've shot my ass off if her finger tripped the trigger.

"Why are they important to you?" She looked to Maceo who was speaking on the phone, asking the obvious question.

I hadn't explained their connection with Wu. It was something I planned on explaining later, but I trusted Clara with all my secrets.

"Their father is a major player in Thailand, both a business mogul and mob boss. His daughter was the one I killed."

Her eyes rounded. "Josh, you're kidding."

"I wish I were." I gestured toward the door. "His sister is somewhere in there. Or at least I hope. I'm not leaving without them both."

"I've got your back."

The three of us entered the desolate mansion using what looked to be the servant's entrance. We passed through a kitchen and a long hallway with a pantry and other storage closets.

"Where do you think she would be?" Clara held her gun with a steady hand, cupping her fist like a pro. Her finger stayed off the trigger. I'd have to ask her later how she knew about guns.

"Maceo, do you know?"

"I haven't seen my sister since they kidnapped us except at the fights, but I know he keeps her in the house. The guards talk about…" His scowl deepened. "They talk about the things he makes her do."

"Okay." I thought it through.

Carson had been a total dick and control freak. He wouldn't put her where he didn't have easy access to the girl. I ruled out a continued search of the downstairs.

"Let's move up."

Not knowing the layout of the house, it would be difficult to search, and any minute that chopper would land. Xavier's crew expected us to be in that parking lot and we weren't going to be there.

"Do we spread out?" Clara asked.

"No fucking way. You stick by my side."

We climbed the stairs, encountering no one. In fact, the entire house seemed abandoned.

A sweeping staircase led to a second level and I took a guess the master suite would be up there. We headed up.

Turning left, we ran across a series of guest rooms. Knowing the size of Carson's ego, I turned everyone around to the opposite wing.

Jackpot!

We located the master suite, but there was no girl.

"Shit." Where could she be?

Clara moved out in front of me, gun level, hands steady. She headed toward the bathroom.

"Hold up." I didn't want her going first.

Maceo stayed behind me, hovering at the door. Outside, the low *whomp—whomp—whomp* of an approaching helicopter made the air vibrate.

We walked into the ornate master bath. Maceo followed behind us. He clutched the phone in his hand, no longer speaking to whoever was on the other end. His cagey eyes swept back and forth. To either side, two doors led to what I assumed were walk-in closets.

"Malee?" Maceo called out. "Are you here?"

A muffled noise came from the door to our left. I wanted to shout at Maceo to wait, but he rushed the door and practically took it off its hinges as he flung it open.

As he crashed through, I followed. Chained to a wall, Malee knelt on a small pallet. Tears streaked her cheeks and I swallowed against the extensive bruising on her body. A quick glance around the room showed no clothing. I turned around.

"Clara, see if there's anything she can wear." Looking at Clara's half-dressed state, I wanted her covered head to toe. No man would ever again look upon her as a naked slave. The thought churned my stomach.

"Of course." Clara kept her gun up and searched the bathroom.

It occurred to me to tell her not to pick any of Carson's clothes. I wanted none of his filth touching Malee, but I didn't need to worry. Clara returned with a feminine looking floor length robe.

Maceo held his sister and they clutched each other as I went to the wall. No keys meant there was no way to get the manacles off her wrists, but that wasn't a problem. I curled my fingers into a fist and punched at the wall. Of course, the chain had been bolted into a supporting two by four. Maceo got to his feet, and between the two of us, we yanked the anchoring bolts out by brute force.

I turned to Malee. "Can you walk?"

"Yes," she replied in perfect English.

The four of us exited the master suite and pulled up short at the sound of men moving on the floor below. I waved everyone back and took a look over the railing.

Chambers, Abrams, Bay, Chad, and two other men I didn't know were decked out in black tactical gear and armed to the hilt. They swept the area below with their guns.

"Up here," I called out.

"What the fuck, Davenport?" Chambers lowered his weapon. "What part of meet us at the rendezvous point did you not understand? And who the fuck was on the phone?"

"Whatever." I gestured to Clara and the twins. "You're going home."

Maceo clutched his sister and she wept on his shoulder. I knew the horrors these children suffered at Carson's hands, but they wouldn't have suffered at all if Wu had simply given in to Carson's demands and handed over his territory. Wu was as much at fault for what happened to his children as Carson.

His son had been turned into a killer and his daughter had been subjected to rape and worse.

In this, it was difficult to judge who was the bigger monster. Except to say, for the first time in a very long time, that man wasn't me.

Chapter 12

Josh

CHAMBERS AND THE OTHERS SURROUNDED CLARA AND WU'S children. I stayed right in front of Clara, protecting her as best I could. Chambers and his team led us out of the mansion to the waiting helicopter.

"We can't take the kids." Chambers shouted over the noise of the rotors.

"We're not leaving them."

"This isn't a part of the plan."

"Not your plan. Those two are coming with us."

Chambers pursed his lips, but I wasn't going to budge.

"It's not up for discussion," I said.

"We don't have the weight allowance for two more."

"Sure you do." I glanced in the helicopter. There was seating for eight. Damn, he was right, then I had an idea. "Leave two of your guys behind."

"Like hell I will."

I pointed to the back buildings. "There's about two dozen boys and girls back there who are scared as shit and could use a little help. They have no one and nowhere to go. Send your guys to help them. Get them someplace safe."

Chambers scratched the back of his head, then exchanged words with Abrams. The two of them stepped away, while Clara climbed into the helicopter with the twins.

After a short discussion and a call back to Xavier, Chambers spoke with his men. Chad, Bay, and the two new men set off at a jog toward the buildings.

"Get in," Chambers said, "we're taking you to the jet."

"And what about them?"

"Xavier is working on it."

Clara and Malee sat in the center seats. Malee's brother put his arm around his sister and spoke into her ear. Clara glanced at me, kept her hands in her lap, and still had a grip on that revolver with perfect gun etiquette with her finger off the trigger.

I kept my head down and climbed on board. Chambers and Abrams followed and sat opposite the boy and girl. They leaned forward and helped the teens with the webbed restraints, making sure they were safe and secure. I did the same for Clara and slowly eased the revolver out of her hand and tucked it beneath my waistband.

She clutched my hand as the helicopter tilted forward and we took off. The deafening chop of the rotors made communication impossible, so I simply sat and held her hand.

We landed less than a half an hour later at the airport where a jet waited to take us back to Xavier's island. Once clear of the helicopter, it lifted off again and headed back the way we had come. Chambers and Abrams stayed with us.

"Let's get everyone on board." Chambers tried ushering us onto the plane, but I shook my head.

"I need to make a phone call."

"We need to get out of here."

Wu made me memorize the number to a burner phone. He refused to allow me to program it into my contacts. With his assets, he would have a team prepped and ready to pick up his kids, but was it safe to wait here?

I altered my plans. Xavier may give me shit for it later, but I really didn't give a damn. My conversation with Wu was short and to the point.

When I got on the plane, I checked in on the twins, making sure they were okay. The girl huddled beside her brother and refused to speak to anyone but him.

"We're good," Maceo said. "What happens now?"

"We're taking you home."

Chambers gave me a look which I ignored. I brushed by him and headed to the cockpit.

"We're diverting," I told the lead pilot.

"Our instructions are to return——" Chambers argued.

"I don't give a damn. We're taking those two to their father."

"I'll have to call this in."

"Don't bother." I pulled out my phone and had another short conversation with Xavier. To my surprise, he didn't resist.

"Put the pilot on the phone," Xavier said.

I handed the phone to the pilot, then returned to where Clara waited. Plopping down beside her, I let out a sigh.

"We're taking you home."

Maceo glanced up. "Thank you."

"What's going on?" Chambers stripped out of his combat gear, pulling clips from belt loops and storing his weapons in a secure box. Abrams worked beside him, but said nothing the entire time.

"We're making a short diversion."

"Does Xavier know about this?"

"Of course, he does." These men did nothing without express permission from Xavier. "Have you heard anything about the other kids?"

"Chad radioed in. They have them. Transportation is inbound."

"Thank fuck for that."

I could sleep well knowing Marcus and the others wouldn't fall prey to other villainous men on the streets. Xavier's team would take care of the kids.

At a signal from the pilot, Chambers and Abrams secured the plane for takeoff.

"You should get some rest." Clara snuggled against me. "It's been a long day."

Adrenaline spiked in my veins and buzzed along my nerves. There was no way I would be sleeping.

"Lay your head on my shoulder." I kissed the top of her head. "You were amazing."

"No. You were. You're a hero."

I didn't know about that.

Before we reached altitude, Clara slept soundly with her head on my shoulder. The twins spoke softly amongst themselves while Chambers and Abrams played cards. I sat and closed my eyes, unable to sleep, but needing rest.

I wasn't looking forward to my upcoming meeting with Wu. If I brought his children home, I might live, but I doubted his promise. I had killed his eldest. In a culture where saving face meant more than forgiveness, he was obligated to take my life.

We landed a few short hours later and Clara stretched beside me. My chest tightened and I sucked in a deep breath. This next part wouldn't be easy.

I had made a decision during the flight.

One Clara would not appreciate.

Chapter 13

Clara

"What do you mean I can't go with you?" I stamped my foot and couldn't believe what Josh said.

"You will return to Xavier's island."

"But I want to go with you."

There was a look in his eyes, one which I didn't like. It had the sense of goodbye and I felt as if I was losing him.

"Clara," he placed a hand on my arm, "you can't come with me."

"Why?" I searched his expression, trying to decide why this felt like the end. "You promise you'll come back, right?"

He never made a promise he couldn't deliver.

"Please don't make a scene, and don't fight me on this. Wu is not a man I want you anywhere near."

But he'd let me kneel naked next to Carson? Who was this Wu? Something in my gut said this was wrong, but the determined look on Josh's face told me this wasn't a conversation I would win.

We'd landed a few minutes ago and the plane had taxied off the runway. Soon, we would come to a stop. I was losing him.

He took my hands in his and leaned in, pressing our foreheads together. "I love you. Never forget how much I love you. You made me into a better man. You don't know what that means to me."

"Well, it means you better come back to me." I squeezed his hands. "Promise me."

He pulled back and took a moment to stare at me. It felt as if he were memorizing my face. Saying goodbye.

"No." I shook my head.

"Clara..." he warned.

"I won't go unless you promise."

He leaned forward and brushed his lips over mine.

Chambers opened the door and lowered the stairs to the ground. Outside a sleek SUV waited and two men in black stood guard outside the car.

"I have to go." He kissed me.

It was both far too short and yet felt as if it lasted an eternity.

"I love you," I said.

"I love you more." He turned and gestured to the twins. "Are you ready?"

The twins looked rough, battered, bruised and broken. They held each other's hand as they walked out of the airplane. I stayed inside with Chambers while Abrams exited the plane behind Josh.

"He'll be back," Chambers said. "That man loves you."

"Then why did that feel like goodbye?"

The twins climbed into the SUV. Josh stood with his hand on the door and looked back to the plane. I waved to him as he slipped inside and shut the door.

Tears welled up in my eyes, but I refused to let them fall. This wasn't goodbye, and therefore there was no reason to cry. I had to believe that.

Abrams returned and closed the door to the plane, sealing us inside.

"We have a few minutes while we refuel," Chambers said, "you should get some rest."

My body had no idea what time it was. From the faint glow on the horizon, dawn was fast approaching, but I didn't know what time zone we were in or what time zone we were headed to.

Less than an hour later, we were back in the air. I sat alone and stared out the window as the sun crested above the clouds. Sometime later, I was being gently shaken awake.

"We're landing." Chambers stood over me.

Abrams was asleep toward the front of the plane. After making sure I was up, Chambers went to wake his friend. We landed and taxied to a stop. The last time I had come here, there had been a blindfold over my head.

I guessed its absence meant I'd been welcomed into the inner circle.

But what kind of circle did that entail?

These were not Josh's friends; therefore, they weren't mine.

Chapter 14

Josh

THE RIDE TO WU'S ESTATE OCCURRED IN SILENCE. MALEE CRIED ON and off. Maceo tried his hardest to remain strong for his sister, but I could see the cracks forming the closer we got. This boy had been forever altered by his ordeal. Not that his sister hadn't suffered, but she had been a victim. Maceo was a victim too, but he had been presented with a choice.

Live or die.

And that did things to a person. I knew.

I lived it.

He would need to learn how to live with the truth within him.

When we approached the iron gates of Wu's estate, I turned to Maceo. His outer shell was already beginning to crack. The two guards sat up front.

"You did what you had to do to survive."

His glassy eyes turned to me with the precursors of tears. If this boy broke down in front of his father, it would be a mistake he would never recover from.

"Malee is safe because of you. She's here…because of you."

"I did nothing—"

"You did everything. She's here, isn't she?"

He looked at me. Stared at me. And slowly, he understood.

The fear and agony…the pain and suffering…he shoved all of it deep inside of himself, swallowing it down with a maturity he should never have found. It took a moment, but he found his center, then he looked at me with inquisitive eyes.

"Who are you?"

There was no reason to lie to the boy. He would know soon enough.

"I'm the one who killed your sister."

My words were absorbed with a slow blink.

"What are you doing here?"

"I'm repaying a debt."

"Why aren't you dead?"

"Because your father decided my life still had value."

"You saved us."

I had, but this boy didn't need to listen to me preen.

"I was there for another reason." My hand patted the pocket of my pants and the cellphone I hoped would help Xavier and Forest with whatever it was they had planned.

"But you saved us."

"You saved Malee. I was just in the right place at the right time."

"And yet you're bringing us to our father? He will kill you."

"He has that right."

We said nothing further as the ornate wrought iron gates slowly drew open. The SUV pulled between the massive gates, and we slowly approached Wu's estate.

He was not outside to greet us.

The guards opened the doors for us. Malee stepped out with her brother shielding her from pretty much everything. I think she was the only thing keeping him in one piece.

The thin robe covering her nakedness blew in the slight breeze and the faintest scent of tropical flowers filled the air, reminding me of Xavier's estate and the garden guarding the border between his house and the beach.

I had freed Clara on that beach and found my peace there as well. Whatever my future held, I would always have that memory.

The three of us were instructed to head inside. I found that odd, considering this was the twin's home. They proceeded me up the marble steps. Twin doors, sculpted by the finest woodsmiths, opened wordlessly as we approached.

Maceo held his sister as he ushered her inside.

Standing in the ornate foyer, Wu stood with his feet spread apart and his arms crossed over his chest. He said nothing, keeping his expression solemn, until the doors closed behind us. Then, it was as if a switch flipped inside of him.

The cold, calculating businessman and mob boss disappeared. Arms outstretched, he beckoned his children into his embrace.

I stood there with the guards, awkwardly trying not to intrude on what was a private moment, and unable to leave.

Malee buried her face against her father's chest and sobbed. Maceo wrapped his arm around his father and placed his forehead against his father's shoulder. They stood there for what seemed like forever before Wu whispered into his daughter's ear and said something to his son.

Maceo looked to me.

Wu gave them a hug and then ushered them up the sweeping staircase. Maceo took his sister's hand in his and slowly led her up to the private areas of the estate.

This left me, Wu, and his two guards flanking me with nowhere to run. Not that I would. My fate resided in this man's hands.

"You brought my children back to me."

"I brought Malee and Maceo back to you. Unfortunately, they are no longer children."

"I understand."

"I'm sorry."

"You can't be sorry for returning what is precious to me."

"I wasn't speaking about the twins."

"I see." He gave a slow nod, then gestured toward a study to his left. "Please, we have business to discuss."

I didn't want to discuss any business with Wu. He was my path to freeing the hooks Kate and Lily sank into me when they took my money. I didn't want to exchange those for any ties to Wu.

Dammit.

I wanted the freedom to choose my path.

Lead a simple life.

I wanted to breathe.

When the guards tried to follow us inside the study, Wu waved them off and closed the doors himself.

"Please?" He gestured to a chair facing an ornate mahogany desk.

I took the seat and prepared for whatever might come next.

"I want to thank you again for saving my children."

"I'm afraid I didn't save them."

"They will receive the best counseling available to deal with the aftermath."

Of that, I had no doubt, but counseling couldn't fix what those kids had endured.

"Which," Wu continued, "brings me to what to do with you."

"I told you I would bring your children back."

"Because you wanted to erase your debt?" His brow lifted.

"I can never repay my debt. I took the life of your daughter. There is no payment which can erase that."

"I agree. Which makes this an awkward conversation."

Honor demanded he take my life. An eye for an eye and a life for a life. There was no way I was walking out of here alive.

"If I let you live, it will send the wrong message to my enemies."

"They will think you're weak."

"True, and yet I find myself indebted to you."

"There is no debt."

"You say that, but you also once told me you sought redemption. Tell me, why should I allow a man like you to live?"

"Well..." I shifted in the seat and leaned forward. "I'd like to tell you a story."

"A story?"

"About a man who had nothing to live for until he had everything to lose."

"I'm listening."

I began at the beginning, back in my high school days when Jake and Kevin and I had been the best of friends, before I met Wu's daughter, and didn't stop until I reached the end.

My voice broke when I recounted the night of my arrest; the night my father tried to force me to torture and rape Kate Summers, the night he told me to murder the woman my brother loved. I told him about my release from prison and the moment I first set eyes on Clara. I ended with three words.

"I love her."

"I respect that." Wu pinched at his chin. "But there's still the matter of your death."

Chapter 15

Clara

It had been three days without any word from Josh. My entire existence felt disconnected, like I was waiting in a bubble where time didn't exist. Any moment, I expected Josh to turn a corner in one of the many endless halls of Xavier's estate, or emerge from the tropical gardens and step onto the beach.

I would look up and he would smile. Then I'd be running. Flying into his arms. We would embrace. Our kiss would be epic. And he would twirl me in a huge circle. His eyes would light up and a smile would fill his face.

I thought about that at least a hundred times a day.

And I did run into him, or rather his identical twin. Each time, my heart did a double take once it realized the vision in front of me was not *My Monster* but rather another man.

Those moments inevitably drove me out to the cove. Which was where I found myself on whatever day of the week this happened to be.

I had a book in my hand and an umbrella shading my fair skin from the tropical sun. The slight lapping of waves as they washed up on the pristine, white sands of the protected cove provided a soothing backdrop to the romance novel I tried to read.

I hated everything about it. The beach. The sun. The waves. And most importantly, the love story I couldn't seem to read.

There was no one to share it with.

Not that there weren't people around me. Chambers, inevitably, hovered. Since I was no longer a slave, his duties as my guard had been lifted, but he always seemed to find a reason to be around me.

I ran into him nearly as much as I ran into Jake.

Jake with the same smoldering jade-green eyes as Josh.

Fortunately, Jake and Kate chose not to join me on the beach today.

Since I'd dressed Kate down, she hovered as well, constantly apologizing for what she had done. Forgiving her had been an act of kindness. I wouldn't hold a grudge against the only family Josh had, even if his brother refused to speak to him.

We would have a conversation about that the next time I saw Jake. He needed to get his head out of his ass about the past.

Josh had suffered enough and gone above and beyond in seeking redemption. He'd never ask his brother's forgiveness, but damn if I wouldn't force Jake to do the right thing.

A gust of wind ruffled the mirror-smooth water as it blew in off the ocean. It lifted tiny grains of sand which covered me in a fine grit. I shook out the pages of the book and lost my place. Not that I'd been paying attention to what I read.

Chambers had set up his spot down the beach from mine. He said he was just kicking it on the beach. Raven and her two guards had joined me earlier. She invited me to go snorkeling, but I wasn't interested. I didn't want to be out there if Josh decided to show up.

The trio disappeared beneath the crystal blue waters, decked out in their dive gear, about half an hour ago, intent on exploring the coral reefs. I sat with my book, shading my eyes against the brilliance of the sun.

For the thousandth time, my thoughts drifted to Josh.

Where was he?

What was he doing?

Why hadn't he come back?

A quick glance down at the page and I realized I had no idea what I had just read. It wasn't a mystery thriller, but rather a romance; an entire genre I stopped reading while held as Josh's slave.

What I wouldn't give to return to that room. Things had been black and white. Rules were followed. Consequences enforced. There had been an incredible simplicity to my existence which I missed.

You don't miss that room, idiot. And you definitely don't miss those stupid rules.

You're right. I miss him. But I kind of miss the rules too.

I didn't care what path had brought us together. Josh did terrible things, but he wasn't a horrible person. In him, I saw a man willing to put everything at risk to save others.

A shadow fell over the sand in front of me and someone blocked the sun. My heart did a little flip, at least until I stared up at the stranger.

"May I sit down?"

Holy Viking glory! The man was something out of Norse mythology.

Shock-white hair. Glacial eyes. Thighs the size of tree trunks. A neck stacked with muscle, and we weren't even going to talk about the hardened planes of his chest and abs.

The man terrified me. At least until he smiled. No one deserved a smile that pure. It put me instantly at ease because I felt I could trust this man.

"Um…who are you?" In my short time at Xavier's estate, I'd never seen him.

"My name is Forest." He extended a massive bear-sized hand. "Forest Summers."

"Um…" I glanced to where Chambers straightened his towel farther down the beach. He watched me, but made no move to interfere. I took that as a sign he knew Forest.

"I promise…" Forest flashed that megawatt smile again, "I don't bite."

"It's just…"

"I get it. But don't let it fool you."

"What?"

"My size. My sister calls me her little beanpole."

"Um, Xavier keeps an unusual crop of friends. Who's your sister?"

"Skye. She was the doc…" He looked at me as if the connection was obvious. Then I remembered the medical team.

"So, are you a friend of Xavier's?"

"I'm not sure yet. I haven't decided if he's worthy."

"What does that mean?"

I didn't know what was different about this man, but an awkwardness hung all over him. It was as if he didn't know how to interact with me.

Or maybe it was in the way he studied me, like I was under a microscope with all my actions catalogued and compared against a playbook of scripted responses.

He was friendly, but half a step behind the social reactions I expected.

"People confuse me. I guess you could say Xavier is becoming a friend, but we're really more business associates."

"Oh, were you involved in…" I stopped myself, unsure about revealing secrets I shouldn't say.

"You're smart, Clara." He pointed to a spot beside me. "Do you mind if I share your shade? We have something to talk about." His smile flattened and turned serious.

"I guess it's okay." Another glance toward Chambers and I felt safe allowing this imposing man into my personal space.

"First, I want to thank you."

"Me?"

"Because of you, I have something I've been searching for."

"What's that?"

"The key."

The man spoke in riddles.

"I don't understand."

"I'm not really good at this."

"This?"

He gave a low rumble of a laugh. "The talking to pretty girls."

"A man with your looks? I bet you have women falling at your feet."

"It happens, but I'm uncomfortable with what comes next. Men are simpler. Easier to understand. Not to mention, they don't break."

That comment left me stumbling for how to respond.

"Anyway," he continued, "you've helped me; my sister and I."

"I still don't understand?"

"Zane Carson worked for a man I've spent my entire life trying to track down."

"Snowden?" I had heard that name dropped in conversation.

"I understand you were at the fights?"

"I was." A shudder rippled through me. "It was…"

"Supposed to be me."

"Excuse me?"

"My sister and I were foster kids together and Snowden…" His voice cracked and choked on Snowden's name. "He planned on… well…Let's just say, that very well could have been me in that ring. I didn't look like this back then. There's a reason Skye calls me her beanpole."

My eyes widened with realization. "How old were you?"

"Seventeen."

That seemed old considering the ages of the boys we'd rescued.

"He was going to kidnap you?"

"I don't know if kidnap is the right word. He paid to take us off our foster father's hands. Me for the fights and Skye…"

"I'm so sorry." How long ago had that been? Forest had to be in his late twenties or early thirties. "How long have you been searching for Snowden?"

"It's been a minute or two." He evaded my question. "Anyway, what was done to you wasn't right, and I don't know how to apologize except to say I'm sorry."

"It seems that's all anyone around here does."

"What's that?"

"Apologize."

"It was wrong."

"Agreed, but Josh…" Tears shimmered in my vision. "He's not what any of you think. He's not a monster."

"Xavier told me you care for him." He cocked his head, looking genuinely confused. "I'm surprised. I would think you would hate him." He looked suddenly uncomfortable.

"I hear that all the time too, but you don't know him like I do. He's kind, caring, and…"

"You love him." Forest said it not as a question, but as a statement of fact. "I'll be damned, another Lover Boy." A twinkle sparkled in his glacial gaze, like he shared some private joke with himself.

"Have you heard anything?" I desperately needed to know and Forest seemed involved. If he and Xavier worked together, maybe Forest could help me figure out when Josh would be back.

"I came to discuss what happens next. It's time for you to move on."

"Until Josh returns, I'm staying right here. He's my next step."

"You can't stay here forever. My foundation has prepared everything you need for your new life."

"My new life is with Josh."

His full lips pressed together and he refused to look me in the eye.

"Unfortunately, until we bring Snowden down, your life is in danger, an unavoidable consequence, but we've established a new identity, the finest training is available for you, a degree if you want it, whatever you want actually. We'll make it happen. My plane is leaving this afternoon, and you'll be coming with me. Xavier's orders."

"I'm not leaving until Josh returns." They would have to drag me kicking and screaming.

"About Josh," he still refused to look at me.

"What about him?"

"I'm sorry, but he didn't make it."

"What do you mean he didn't make it?"

"Clara." His voice shifted vocal registers and headed into dangerous overtones, "Josh is dead."

Chapter 16

Josh

THERE HAD BEEN NO DISCUSSION AND NO NEGOTIATION. AS MUCH AS I hated to admit it, I had to die.

Wu offered a choice.

I could walk out of his home with my identity wiped or leave as Joshua Davenport. His men were obligated to avenge the wrongs committed against their boss and would track me down in a bid to garner favor with him.

Allowing the man who murdered his daughter to walk free made him appear weak to his enemies.

But he couldn't kill me.

Not after I saved the lives of his children. That made him appear ungrateful, and a man who refused to repay a life-debt had a very short lifespan within his social circles.

It was complicated.

We agreed.

Joshua Davenport died the night I brought his children home.

But it took a few days.

First, word got out that Wu found the man who had killed his eldest daughter. There was the requisite waiting period where he extracted his pound of flesh. That couldn't be faked, and I spent two days in his basement getting the shit kicked out of me. There needed to be indisputable proof of death, and we provided that in a broadcast of my torture to his associates.

I took time to recover.

Over the next two weeks, I underwent subtle reconstructive surgery. Nothing major, just enough to alter my appearance so that facial recognition couldn't match my old face with my new face.

Two days of torture. Two weeks of recovery. Two months of living hell. I barely recognized myself.

I died several times over during that process because I lost what meant the most to me.

But I would make amends.

I couldn't be with Clara. It was simply too dangerous to ask her to live a life with me, but I could ensure she lived a life without want.

Wu saw to this as well. It had been a part of our original agreement.

I found myself with a new identity and a bank account with more than enough zeroes to begin a new, comfortable, life.

I gave it all to Clara. Hell, she deserved it far more than me.

Our forever vanished the night of the fight and it was something we would both have to live with. Knowing how Forest and Xavier operated, I had no doubt they had already set her up with a new life and new identity.

I found myself in the Cayman Islands, sitting at a bank associate's desk, waiting for him to verify the funds in my account. Jake and Kate could have the millions they took from me. Hopefully, they put them to good use.

I kicked back and aimlessly drew hearts on the armrest of the chair with my finger. A presence loomed to my left and I glanced up.

I knew that face.

"What the fuck are you doing here?"

If Forest found me, who else would do the same?

Shit.

"Relax, Lover Boy, your secret is safe with me."

"How did you find me?"

"I have a talent for finding lost things."

"I'm not lost."

"I suppose you're not, but I know someone who is."

Clara.

My heart skipped a beat.

Once I secured the funds in the transfer account, they would all be wired to an account I set up for her. I didn't have any use for it, but she earned every damn penny with the shit I'd put her through.

"You're going to be fucking noble, I see." Forest took the seat beside me, folding his large frame into the chair. "I was wondering what your play would be. I expect the money in your account will soon belong to another?"

I wasn't going to play games with him, and he still hadn't answered my question.

"How the fuck did you find me?"

Wu and I worked hard to make certain Joshua Davenport disappeared.

"Like I said, I have skills."

"Well, what the fuck do you want?"

"For starters, to say thank you. For seconds, to ask for your help."

"Is that all?"

"Not really. You know how everything comes in threes? In this case, the third thing is one rather bothersome woman."

"You sure as shit better not be telling me you brought Clara here."

"Okay, I won't say a word. And I didn't bring her here. She won't leave me alone. Refuses to leave my side until I find you."

"Find me?"

"Yeah, evidently she believes you're not dead. Even after she saw the footage." Forest winced. "That was some brutal shit."

"You shouldn't have brought her."

"Like I said, I didn't. Your girl is tenacious as shit."

"Where is she?"

"Back at the resort."

I vaulted to my feet. "You fucking bastard."

My shout turned heads and Forest shook his, as if he had the right to judge me.

"You two clearly belong together. And she sure as shit won't let me do anything for her. She refuses everything. No new life. No new identity. She threatened to make a martyr of herself and broadcast to the world who she was. I think she has a death wish, and between you and me, I'm tired of keeping her safe from herself. She's your problem because she sure as shit won't listen to me."

The associate returned, which silenced my conversation with Forest. He tucked his hands in his lap while the associate asked for my unique identifier and code.

That's all it took. Ten million dollars flew through the Ethernet into a bank account I had set up for Clara.

Fucking Forest brought her to the Caymans.

So damn close.

Once I concluded my business, I was on my feet and headed to the door.

"Don't you want to know what resort we're staying at?" Forest called out from behind me.

"Don't need to. You're taking me to her."

"Well, thank fuck for that, and here I thought I'd have to drag you kicking and screaming."

"Stop that shit and take me to Clara."

Forest lifted his arm over his head. A block away, a white SUV pulled from the curve. It stopped in front of us.

"After you," Forest said.

I practically launched inside the car. I was that eager.

It had been months since I'd seen Clara, yet it felt as if it had been longer than a lifetime. I thought she was lost to me. Honestly, I had tried to convince myself she would be better off without me. Even if I knew…I fucking knew…that wasn't true.

"Tell me what happened." I tugged the seatbelt across my body and buckled in.

"We got news Wu killed you—pretty convincing by the way—and I was the one who broke the news to Clara. She insisted on watching by the way. I wasn't going to show her. Let's just say it didn't go over well. Xavier and I had to practically drag her off the island. She wouldn't leave, so damn convinced you'd return any moment. I took her to our rehabilitation facilities and tried to set her up in the program. She refused, saying she knew you wouldn't leave her, that you wouldn't die, and that she was going to wait for you."

"Shit." I ran my palm over my face.

"I don't know about that, but definitely a unique brand of crazy. She had me believing you might actually still be alive, which led to a little search, which led down one hell of a rabbit hole, which led me here."

"Wu's associates will hunt me down if they learn I'm still alive. They owe it to him to avenge his honor."

"Oh, you're dead. Joshua Davenport is dead as a doorknob."

"Then how…"

"How did I find you?"

"Yeah."

"Persistence, and I'm kind of a sucker for love. Lord knows how many times I've had to give it a little nudge here and there. Skye's hubby needed one hell of a push, and then there were the others."

We pulled up to a five-star resort. Valets swarmed the car, opening both my door and Forest's, in what could only be called choreographed perfection. Once out of the car, I turned to him.

"Where is she?" He glanced up at the sun, as if judging the time by its position in the sky.

"About this time, I'm guessing she's at the beach. Your girl has a rather eclectic reading collection."

I took off at a jog.

"Don't you want to know *where* she is, Lover Boy?"

It was a beach. How damn big could it be?

Turns out, pretty fucking huge. There had to be over a hundred chairs lined up for the guests. About a third were occupied. A score of cabanas lined the back of the beach and nearly all of those had people in them.

But no Clara.

What the ever-loving fuck?

My heart raced. My fingers tingled. Forest wouldn't lie. But where was Clara?

Think!

I needed to be systematic, and shit if the sun wasn't hot. I'd dressed in linen trousers and a loose-fitting cotton shirt, perfect island attire, but not for a damn beach.

I kicked off my shoes and rolled up the cuffs of my pants and then began at one end of the beach area owned by the resort. By the time I hit the third row of chairs, people were starting to stare. I turned the scowl on my face into a smile, which seemed to help a little.

Sweat trickled down my back and plastered my shirt to my skin. Frustrated, I tugged it off and received a whole new chorus of stares from the women on the beach. The few men barely registered my presence.

I was on the last row, and there was no sign of Clara. There were a few beach chairs with stuff but no occupants, but I'd already searched the water. I didn't know how much of a swimmer Clara might be, but she wasn't chilling off in the ocean.

Putting my hand to the back of my neck, I shielded my eyes from the sun. Would she be in one of the cabanas? That didn't seem to be her style, but it did seem like something Forest would do.

Again, starting on the left, I began my search. It didn't take long before I drew the attention of the attendants as I poked my head into each and every cabana. They started to close in on me, probably to politely ask if they could help me, but I saw the radio calls they made.

Two large men wearing pink polos stamped with *Security* were making a beeline toward my position.

I'd already startled one mother as she lathered her children with sunscreen. I popped open the curtain on another couple surprising them mid-coitus. There was the rich bastard showing off his wealth to a bevy of girls who barely looked legal.

"Sir?" Shit, one of the little attendants was closing in. I poked my head into the next cabana, but it was empty.

"Sir? May I help you?" The young man picked up his pace, trying not to kick sand on the guests as he trotted to catch up to me.

Ignoring him, I moved on to the next cabana. An old battered copy of *The Phantom Tollbooth* sat on the lounger. I gripped one of the poles and took in a breath as my heart slammed into my throat.

I'd found her. A hand fell on my shoulder.

"Sir, the cabanas are for hotel guests only. Are you a guest?"

One of the security guards had caught up to me. The tiny male attendant looked comical standing next to him.

"No."

"Sir, I'll have to ask you to leave."

I shrugged off his hand and glared at him. He took half a step back before he realized what he'd done. We stood eye to eye matched in height and bulk, but I had something he didn't. Perhaps he sensed the menace radiating off me, but he had a job to do.

"No need to do this, man," I said, trying to diffuse what could easily become an ugly situation. "I'm a guest of Mr. Summers." I didn't know if a guard would be privy to the names of the VIP guests, but I figured it was worth a shot.

The guard didn't know, but the attendant certainly did.

"Sir, will Mr. Summers be joining you?" It was a polite way of saying he needed to verify my story, but wouldn't make a scene in the off-chance I was telling the truth.

"I doubt it." This gave the two of them pause, but I didn't let them stew about it too long. "The woman who's sitting here. Where is she?"

"I'm sorry, sir, but we can't give out information about our guests."

"Look, I get you're doing your job, but I'm not leaving until she returns."

The security man puffed out his chest and I rolled my eyes. I didn't have time for this shit.

"If you would come with me, we can verify—" The dick in a pink polo shirt made a grab for my arm.

"We're not verifying shit. Tell me where she is."

The attendant's Adam's apple bobbed, and he looked to the

man beside him for help. Clearly, they weren't going to budge. I'd call Forest and have him run interference, but I had no one's number.

Not Forest's.

Not Xavier's.

Not even my brother's.

Cutting all ties, and disappearing from the world, meant amputating anything connected with that life, even Clara.

I was fucked if I didn't think of something quick because the asshole in the pink shirt's backup was jogging toward us to back him up.

Then I heard the sweetest sound on earth.

"Josh?"

Chapter 17

Clara

I KNEW THAT ASS, THAT TRIM WAIST, AND THE SCULPTED MUSCLES OF that back and those shoulders which carried such heavy burdens.

Josh was a chiseled, sculpted, masterpiece of perfection and he was here.

"Josh?" His name tumbled from my lips as a question, but there was no doubt in my heart.

Two of the resort's security detail flanked him and one nervous looking cabana boy shuffled to the side, looking lost and uncertain. They all turned to look at me and I nearly dropped my fruity drink.

I could have had the cabana boy fetch it for me, but I'd forgotten a book in my room. The well-worn copy of the graphic novel, *The Watchmen*, was sandwiched between my arm and my side, and it nearly tumbled to the ground.

Josh turned around and his eyes widened. Then he launched forward, sprinting to my side. The drink went flying, spraying all over the man standing beside me; Josh's twin brother, Jake. *The Watchman* fell to the sand, but I didn't care.

I was flying.

Josh had me in his arms, clutched tight to his chest, and he twirled us in a circle as his lips crashed down on mine. We said nothing. We couldn't. Not with our lips locked together.

Jake edged near us and retrieved the book from the ground, shaking out the sand. He took a step back, giving us space.

Josh's hand slid along the small of my back and down to cup my ass. Pulling me against him, he let me know exactly how he felt. The kiss turned frantic, all consuming. The only sound was the rushing of our breaths, my moans, and his deep, lusty groan as he yanked me hard against him.

"I knew it." Tears fell freely down my cheeks. "I knew you weren't dead."

"I've fucking missed you." He said with a possessive growl. "I'm so sorry."

"Just kiss me." My fingers clawed at his neck and dug into the hair at his nape.

I was frantic to feel every bit of him. My lips bruised beneath his kiss, already swollen, but I didn't care. Overcome with need I wrapped my legs around his body, seeking a desperate connection. I locked my ankles around his hips and met each lash of his tongue with an insatiable hunger.

I had forgotten how good it felt to be held in his arms. No, that wasn't the truth. This feeling was one I remembered well. It was the warm embrace of coming home and belonging in the best way possible.

Josh kissed me as if his life depended on it. His tongue swept inside my mouth, chasing mine. He nipped at my lips here and there, driving me insane. He tasted amazing, dark, sensual, and dangerous. Dangerous because I could lose myself in him. And I didn't care.

Josh could have every piece of me. I would hand him everything.

Every nerve inside my body fluttered with excitement. Electricity hummed along my nerves with a *zing* of eager anticipation. I wanted to feel him everywhere, every soft touch, and even the sharp sting of pain only he could deliver. I closed my eyes and imagined how that might go and the choice I made in that moment.

The outside world disappeared as we reconnected, but I was acutely aware that we were on a public beach. There were also a few questions I needed answered before this went too far.

When he let me up for air, I took the opportunity to punch him in the gut. My hand connected with solid muscle and I shook it out.

"Ow!"

He laughed. God, I missed that laugh. I missed everything about him.

"It's not funny."

He grabbed my hand and massaged it gently.

"You really shouldn't hit me." Something dark swirled in his eyes, something needful and hungry.

"And why not?"

Energy crackled between us, that insane connection forged from a complicated past and fueled by mutual need. His warm breath cascaded over the skin of my neck as he blew into my ear.

"Because, it wakes the beast within me, my sweet Clara. It stirs a hunger, cravings for dark and wicked things. God, I've missed you."

"If you missed me, you wouldn't have disappeared. What the hell happened? Why did you let me think you were dead?"

Why didn't you tell me the truth? I'd lived in agony thinking it might be true.

"Let's not talk about this here." He pressed a finger over my lips. "Is there someplace private we can go?"

"The cabana?" I offered the closest option, but from the lust flaring in his eyes, that was not what he needed.

"Um, my room?"

"That sounds more like it." His hungry gaze swept up and down my body, stripping me with his eyes. I squirmed beneath his attention and squeezed my thighs together to slake the needy throbbing of my sex.

"Let me just get my things."

There was no way I was leaving my books for anyone to steal. I'd paid good money for original copies of the two novels which had kept me sane over the past couple of months.

They kept me connected to Josh.

With them, I traveled between the pages, reminded myself not to jump to Conclusions, and reaffirmed the most insurmountable task began with the smallest steps.

I believed Josh would never abandon me.

That was faith.

I clung to that knowledge with every fiber of my being. Therefore, I refused to believe in his death.

There had to be a reason, some method to the madness, and I may have jumped to the Island of Conclusions too many times to count, but I told Forest that Josh was still alive. He needed to find *My Monster* because I couldn't continue living this way.

I'd been a pain in the ass, but if anyone was going to help me, it was Forest. I told him about Wu and Forest took it from there. He owed me.

They all did.

Especially Jake.

He stood off to the side and I couldn't miss the tension filling the air between him and Josh.

"Hi." Jake's greeting came out tentative and unsure, an odd reaction from the sexual dominant, but he seemed uncertain greeting his brother. "You look different."

"Yeah, shit happened."

Jake sized Josh up with a long sweep of his angular gaze. "It's good to see you."

"Is it?"

An insurmountable gulf separated them, but I sensed the fragile beginnings of a new connection.

"Your girl is an interesting woman. She had a thing or two to say to me."

"Is that so?"

"I'm surprised I have any ass left after the ass-ripping she gave me. Your girl has a strong bite."

"That's what I love about her." A smirk tilted the corner of Josh's mouth.

"Look…" Jake ran his hand through his dark hair, pulling at the roots the same way Josh did when he struggled with what to say. Finally, Jake extended his hand. "It's really good to see you."

Josh's eyebrows practically climbed up his forehead.

"It seems you're not irredeemable…"

"And…" I grabbed Josh's hand and threaded my fingers with his. I'd said a lot of shit to Jake about how he treated his brother, and how he treated me. The things he and Kate did to me were unredeemable, and yet I found it in my heart to forgive them. I had to. Without them, Josh would never have been in my life.

It took several conversations, most filled with my cutting tongue, before I started to get Jake to see an alternate view of what happened.

But this wasn't something I could force. The two of them needed to find each other on their own terms.

"And…" Jake said, "I'm sorry."

Josh took his hand and the two men shook. It looked like that was all they were going to do, but Jake suddenly tugged Josh to his chest and wrapped both arms around his brother.

My Monster hesitated, but then his arms wrapped around Jake. They stood in silence for a moment, then released each other and took an awkward step back.

"I don't understand why you're here? I get Forest, but why you?"

"Someone had to watch over your girl while he went to fetch you. It was the least I could do."

There was more to it than that. I had had *very* stern words with both Kate and Jake about Josh. It was my hope some of that may help to bring them back to one another.

As for Forest, he came through, although he told me finding Josh would be a long shot. I hadn't cared because I believed in Josh. He would go through hell and back to get to me.

Jake held out the lovingly used copy of *The Watchmen* to Josh who took it with a smirk.

Josh turned to me. "I love your choice of reading material."

My cheeks heated. He knew me too well. Josh opened the book to a random page and read a few lines. His smile deepened and all the tension in his body seemed to evaporate before my eyes.

"God, I love you." He turned his deep, soulful eyes on me. "I missed you."

"You owe me an explanation." I fisted my hands on my hips.

"I suppose I do, but it's going to have to wait."

I had no argument about that. We collected our things and walked past the stares of too many inquisitive people. Inside the resort, we made a beeline for the elevators.

As soon as the elevator doors opened, he whisked me inside, and I gave a startled yelp as he thrust me against the back wall. Before I could tell him what floor to push, his lips were on me…again.

He tasted like forever as his tongue swept inside my mouth.

"What floor?" he asked, demanding an answer.

I mumbled the answer as his hand slid up my leg and under the flimsy beach wrap I had on. His fingers glided along the edge of my bikini and my knees buckled. The elevator beeped as we moved past each floor and his fingers slipped under my bikini and thrust inside of me.

Breath rushed out of me as he stroked my clit with a Master's touch. My moans escalated and I nearly came right there. But the elevator slowed and the doors opened.

"What room?"

"End of the hall, last door on the left."

I dug out my keycard, and he ripped it from my hand. He lifted me over his shoulder, and I dangled over his back. With his arms locked around my legs, I gave a tiny squeal. His hand came down sharply on my ass.

"Shh…" he said with a snicker. Then he rubbed away the sting on my ass.

I squirmed on his shoulder and he rewarded me with another sharp crack to my ass.

"Ow! That hurts."

"Hmm," he said, "I bet it does."

He marched down the long hall and pressed the keycard to the magnetic lock. He shouldered the door open and set me on my feet. Then he set upon me, fingers ripping at the threads of my bikini top. He tossed the tiny scrap of fabric to the floor.

We tumbled from the door, making a drunken path toward the bed as he stripped me bare. When the backs of my knees hit the foot of the bed, I toppled backward and stared up at him.

His chest heaved, not with exertion, but with the desire to claim what belonged to him. The expression on his face hardened into something I knew all too well.

Welcome home, My Monster.

"Sir?"

His eyes widened. "Clara, you don't…we don't have to…"

I scooted off the bed and went to my knees. Looking up at him, I flicked open the button of his pants and drew the zipper down with a rasp.

His erection jutted against the fabric of his boxers. It took less than a second to free his engorged cock and I looked up at him, both asking permission and letting him know this was okay.

My lips, bruised and swollen from his kisses, pressed together as I waited for him to decide. Then he reached down and gathered the hair at my nape. Guiding my mouth to the head of his cock, he gave the first of what I hoped to be many commands to come.

"Open, my sweet Clara, please *your Monster*."

Our path may have been long and complicated, twisted and wrong, yet it was also beautifully broken and utterly perfect.

And I had a surprise for him.

Nineteen-year-old girls don't have much trouble getting pregnant. Josh and I had enough unprotected sex to make more babies than I could handle.

But that was okay.

I would take just the one for now.

Josh deserved a good life. With me by his side, and our baby growing within me, he could finally have it all.

I wouldn't have it any other way.

I hope you enjoyed Josh and Clara's story.

Josh is, perhaps, one of my favorite characters that I've written to date.

What to read next?

Take a look at The Ties that Bind series, a BDSM novella series.

The first book in this series, Alexa is FREE.

Alexa

Thank you so much!
The END

Please consider leaving a review

I HOPE YOU ENJOYED THIS BOOK AS MUCH AS I ENJOYED WRITING IT. If you like this book, please leave a review. I love reviews. I love reading your reviews, and they help other readers decide if this book is worth their time and money. I hope you think it is and decide to share this story with others. A sentence is all it takes. Thank you in advance!

CLICK ON THE LINK BELOW TO LEAVE YOUR REVIEW

AMAZON

Books by Jet Masters

The DARKER SIDE[1]
Jet Masters is the darker side of the Jet & Ellie writing duo!

Romantic Suspense
Changing Roles Series:
THIS SERIES MUST BE READ IN ORDER.
Book 1: Command Me
Book 2: Control Me
Book 3: Collar Me
Book 4: Embracing FATE
Book 5: Seizing FATE
Book 6: Accepting FATE

HOT READS
A STANDALONE NOVEL.
Down the Rabbit Hole

Light BDSM Romance
The Ties that Bind

EACH BOOK IN THIS SERIES CAN BE READ AS A STANDALONE AND IS ABOUT A DIFFERENT COUPLE WITH AN HEA.

Alexa
Penny
Michelle
Ivy

HOT READS
Becoming His Series
THIS SERIES MUST BE READ IN ORDER.
Book 1: The Ballet
Book 2: Learning to Breathe
Book 3: Becoming His

Dark Captive Romance
A STANDALONE NOVEL.
She's MINE

---

1. Disclaimer: Books previously published under Ellie Masters

About the Author

JET MASTERS is married to Ellie Masters, contemporary romance and romantic suspense authors.

Together, they've written many books. As his stories turned darker, and hers more contemporary, they decided to split out their different pen names, gathering all the darker, edgier, and more sensual stories under Jet's umbrella.

FOR MORE INFORMATION on Jet, you'll do best to follow his adoring wife, Ellie Masters. Jet doesn't do social media, and is happy about that.

elliemasters.com

facebook.com/elliemastersromance
twitter.com/Ellie__Masters
instagram.com/ellie_masters
bookbub.com/authors/ellie-masters
goodreads.com/Ellie_Masters

Connect with Ellie Masters

Website:
elliemasters.com
Amazon Author Page:
elliemasters.com/amazon
Facebook:
elliemasters.com/Facebook
Goodreads:
elliemasters.com/Goodreads
Instagram:
elliemasters.com/Instagram

Dedication

*This book is dedicated to you, my reader.
Thank you for spending a few hours of your time with me.*

Jet

THE END